Schooled by the Cowboy

Christian Contemporary Western Romance

Brush Creek Cowboys Romance, Book 6

Book Six

Liz Isaacson

ISBN-13: 978-1638760863

"Teach me to do thy will; for thou art my God: thy spirit is good; lead me into the land of uprightness."

Psalms 143:10

Chapter 1

Principal Shannon Sharpe was aware of exactly how long the cowboy had been standing at the corner of the building. It was her job to know, and though he'd never done anything, he couldn't keep coming around school grounds and watching.

She'd employed her excellent detective skills to figure out who he was. After all, she didn't want to alienate a parent, but she also couldn't risk the safety of her students and teachers if the man had a restraining order against him or wasn't allowed to see his child.

Thankfully, this cowboy didn't fit any of that. Wasn't married. Had never been married. Had no children.

He'd dated one of her second grade teachers for a brief time last year, and Shannon suspected the poor guy wasn't over beautiful, bubbly, blonde Claire.

Still, she told herself as the children continued to practice their dance festival pieces. *He can't just show up at school and stare. If a parent saw....*

She turned away from the sixth grade class doing the

cha-cha and clicked her way toward the far corner of the building. Her necklaces jangled as her heels made sharp noises against the blacktop. She fiddled with the hummingbird ring on her middle finger as she approached, the only sign of her nerves.

"Sir?" She paused out of his reach and touched her dangly, sparkling earrings.

The man startled as if he hadn't noticed her approach. He had black hair that extended into a pair of sexy sideburns all the way to his chin. His eyes reminded her of her favorite black tea, and his quick smile made her relax her weight onto her right foot.

"Ma'am." He swept his cowboy hat off and tipped his head in acknowledgement. Shannon wished she was meeting him at one of the town's summer activities, or the community country line dances, or a church function, because he was gorgeous. Tall and broad, with biceps that showed his muscles when he folded them across his chest.

"Can I ask what you're doing here?" she asked, her voice betraying her frantically beating heart. She told herself she would never react like this to a parent, but she already knew this man didn't fit that bill. So her erratic pulse and sudden hopes were justified.

"Oh, I—" His gaze flickered to the open blacktop and back to hers. He seemed to sink into her gaze, and Shannon's hand lifted and pressed against her heart like she was saying the Pledge of Allegiance.

"I've seen you around a few times," she said. "I'm going to have to ask you to leave." True regret lanced through her, because she'd very much like this man to stay, maybe come to her office where she'd close the door and learn more about him. She'd seen him at church with another cowboy from the horse ranch up the canyon and had learned everything she needed to know but his name. And Shannon didn't live in small-town Utah because she disliked cowboys.

Quite the opposite. Problem was, she'd dated every available man during the six years she'd been in Brush Creek, and she'd given up hope of finding someone here. Her disappointment that a transfer hadn't come through this year dried up. Very aware of how unreasonable she was being, she added, "And I think you should stay away. I don't want to have to call the police."

The man fell back a step, alarm entering his eyes. "No need for that. I'll go." He turned and walked away without looking back. A pang of renewed disappointment sang through Shannon, and she sighed as she turned back to the activity on the blacktop. Why did she run off every available man?

It didn't matter. She hadn't gotten a transfer this year, but she'd been at Brush Creek Elementary for six years. Next year would be number seven, and if she didn't get a transfer then, she'd know something was wrong with her performance.

But her parent and teacher surveys had been positive, and she'd never received a negative supervisor evaluation.

With her future almost certainly not in Brush Creek, she didn't need to worry so much about dating. But Shannon also knew she wasn't' getting any younger, and her biological clock seemed to be ticking in her ears louder and louder every day. She wanted a family and children—of her own. Her staff and students had always provided those things for her, and for a while there, Shannon thought that would be enough.

But she knew now that it wasn't. She wanted her own home, her own husband to come home to at night, her own children to cradle and cuddle and cater to.

She swallowed as a fourth grader ran toward her. "Miss Sharpe! Come see our hip hop dance." The excitement on the boy's face brought a smile to Shannon's face, and she moved as quickly as her heels would let her toward the fourth grade group, the pit in her stomach remaining no matter how much she enjoyed the children.

BY THE TIME Shannon finished work for the day, exhaustion consumed her. She unlocked her front door—she was possibly the only person in Brush Creek to lock their door—and exhaled as she entered.

At least she didn't have to come home to darkness and emptiness, as the early May evening still provided sunlight and her two dogs came trotting toward her, seemingly smiling and their tongues hanging out.

"Hey, guys." She put her keys and purse on the front table and bent down to rub her dogs. "Hey, Theo. Did you have a good day?" The curtain at the back of the house fluttered slightly in the wind, an indication that the short-haired Australian shepherd had opened the sliding glass door again.

Her goldendoodle nosed his way into the pat-down, and Shannon chuckled. "All right, Bear. I'll rub you too." The dog flopped on the ground and rolled onto his back, wanting his belly rubbed. "You big baby." She grinned at him, the reason why she locked the front door obvious. Neither of these dogs would bark or scare anyone who tried to break in. And Theo practically invited intruders in by opening the door so he could romp through the backyard.

Shannon straightened and started taking herself apart. First, the earrings came off. She massaged her sore lobes, vowing never to wear that particular pair again as they were too heavy. Then the multiple necklaces. The rings. The business jacket. The heels. Shannon took meticulous care putting every piece in place before she left the house, and it was a relief to just *be* in her own home.

She switched on the television in the living room and moved into the open kitchen to start dinner. She liked to cook just fine, but tonight, she went for easy. And easy meant a mango-peach protein shake on the back patio.

The neighbors were in their backyard and the shouts of children jumping on the trampoline met her ears, along with the scent of grilling hamburgers. Her stomach twisted and roared for meat instead of fruit. Theo and Bear went over to the fence and sat as if someone would accidentally drop a burger over it.

As if drawn by the panting dogs, Shannon's neighbor appeared over the top of the fence. She kept a utility chest there and stood on it when she wanted to talk to Shannon.

"Hey, you are home. Want to come over for dinner?" Ruth was the nicest person on the planet, and Shannon had developed a great friendship with her over the years.

"You don't even have to ask twice." Shannon stood with a grin and added, "Did you make potato salad?"

"Don't I always make potato salad when we have a cookout?"

Shannon grinned, stopped by the kitchen to dump out her uneaten shake, and slipped on some flip flops to go next door. She leashed the two dogs together and told them, "Don't pull. And no jumping," before walking around the fences and through the gate into Ruth's backyard. Her three kids bounced and called on the trampoline in the far corner, and her husband stood at the grill with an overly large spatula.

Ruth lounged in a chair at the patio table, and Shannon joined her, commanding the dogs to sit and wait.

"The dogs can go," she said, and Shannon unleashed them. Theo ran toward the trampoline, more enthralled with play, while Bear made a beeline for Clyde at the grill. The man laughed and rewarded Bear for his loyalty with a corner of bacon.

"Rough week?" Ruth asked, and Shannon opened her eyes. She hadn't even realized she'd closed them.

"May is a rough month," she said. "Everyone's done with school, the principal included." She flashed a weary smile at her friend. "How are things at the hospital?"

"Slow right now, surprisingly." Ruth wasn't wearing her scrubs today, which meant she hadn't worked. But she'd still know.

"That's good, I guess."

"Yeah." Ruth relaxed into her chair, and Shannon appreciated the silence between them on this Friday night.

"So, has Hannah come around?"

Shannon's muscles seized. "No." She didn't mean for

the word to come out like a gunshot, but it still did. "She's still mad at me."

Ruth shook her head and patted her hand. "I'm sorry."

Before last Labor Day, on a rough day like today, after a long week at school, Shannon wouldn't be sitting next door chatting with Ruth. She'd be on the phone with her sister, telling her all about the faculty meeting that had gone over by thirty minutes and the handsome man she'd run off this afternoon.

But Hannah hadn't answered any of Shannon's calls for months. "I honestly thought she'd be over it by now."

"Steve *was* her fiancée," Ruth said.

"Steve was a two-timing jerk who hit on me in my parents' backyard." Shannon set her arms across her chest, her internal organs dancing with apprehension, just like they had been every time she thought of the incident. Every time she relived telling Hannah. Every time she thought about calling her sister—which was everyday—to try to explain one more time.

Shannon had been hit on plenty of times, and she hadn't made a mistake with Steve, no matter what Hannah said. Steve's immediate absence after Shannon's accusations should've backed up her story, but Hannah only blamed her for Steve leaving as well.

Her heart squeezed too tight and she tried to make everything relax by exhaling. It sort of worked.

Ruth copied her and added, "So, no date tonight?"

Shannon groaned. "I'm sorta off men right now, after that last fiasco." She didn't mention the cowboy; hadn't dared to think too much about him at all. If she let herself, she'd find out his name and phone number and call him in for "extra questioning" herself.

"That wasn't a fiasco," Ruth said, having been privy to all the details.

"No? What would you call a man who dates a woman when he already has a girlfriend?"

"Unfortunate?"

Shannon scoffed. "Sure." She didn't want to dwell on the unpleasantness of her most recent attempt at dating. Just because the other woman lived two towns over didn't make her any less of his girlfriend, nor the very public confrontation at the diner any less humiliating. No one had asked Shannon out since, and it had been six months.

Not that Shannon usually let the men ask her out. She almost always made the first move, something she wasn't embarrassed about. She did wonder if sometimes she came off a little too powerful, too strong, too intimidating. She'd been told that in the past, but she wasn't quite sure how not to be like that.

"Heard you were askin' about Grant," Ruth said next, and Shannon sorely regretted this weekend barbeque.

"Who's Grant?" she asked.

"Cowboy up at Brush Creek. Only single one left."

"Black hair? Long sideburns?" Shannon's only hope was to play dumb, like she didn't know who Ruth was talking about.

"That's him."

"He's been hanging around my school," Shannon said. "That's the only reason I was trying to figure out who he was."

"Sure," Ruth said, in the most sarcastic tone possible.

"No really," Shannon insisted. "He was dating one of my teachers last year and clearly isn't over her. Poor guy."

Thankfully, Clyde saved her from having to explain further with an announcement of "Burgers are ready." He set a platter of cheese-topped burgers on the table, and Shannon had to restrain herself from lunging toward them.

At least she could soothe her weariness, her long week, and her loneliness with smoky beef, cheddar, and toasted bread.

CHAPTER 2

Grant arrived back on the ranch at the same time Blake and his family crossed the street to the homestead.

Blake waved at him, pointed to the backyard, and mimed eating. Grant knew exactly what was going down, and he wasn't terribly interested. At the same time, all his cabin had to offer was a stubborn bulldog named Bullseye.

So he cleaned up, put Bullseye's collar on, and opened the back door. The dog took off on his short little legs as Grant vowed not to mention his trip to the elementary school. He'd answered the siren's call of the school several times, and each time he'd left more depressed than the last.

This time was particularly bad, because of that power blonde who'd asked him to leave. Everything about her, from her wavy blonde hair, sharp blue eyes, and miles of accessories screamed polished, and Grant had been impressed. Though their conversation had only lasted a few minutes—and he'd been reprimanded and threatened—he still had enough time to absorb her beauty.

"Don't be stupid," he told himself as he crossed the lane. "That woman is way out of your league."

After all, if a second grade teacher was above him, the principal was in another stratosphere. And he didn't even know the woman's name, though it would be easy enough to find out.

New excitement pooled in his gut as he went around the brick wall fence and into the backyard, where Landon had just placed a steaming sheet tray of steaks on the picnic table. Grant glanced around for the twins, his favorite people since Emmett had gotten married last fall.

He found the almost seven-year-olds on the swing set, their favorite place in the yard.

"Hey," Landon said. "Did you get the—?"

"Yeah, it's in the back of my truck." Grant didn't stop as he moved through the crowd of adults, noting Megan—another possible target if the girls didn't know the name of their principal—and Tess. Justin and Ted and their families weren't there, but Grant assumed they'd arrive soon enough. With the weather finally warming up and the scent of grilled meat in the air, it wouldn't take long for every cowboy to show up at the homestead. And a night where their wives didn't have to cook? Heaven.

Grant wouldn't know, as he'd never been married, and never really been in a serious relationship. All of that was fine while he rode the rodeo circuit, while he tamed bulls and threw ropes and wrestled cattle. He'd only been at Brush Creek for three years, and while he loved it, he'd definitely discovered a widening hole in his life.

"Hey, ladies." He grinned at the girls, who beamed up at him. Rachel launched herself from the swing.

"Uncle Grant!"

He scooped her up, which was much harder than before, and grunted. "Whoa. When did you get so big?"

"I'm almost done with first grade," she announced proudly.

"Is school almost out?" He grinned at her. "What will you do all summer?" He set her down and crouched in front of her. "I know. Bullseye needs a dog-walker. Could you do that?"

"Uncle Grant," Ruby said in a disapproving voice she must've picked up from her mother at some point. "You said *I* could walk Bullseye this summer."

Grant looked at the other girl, who parted her hair on the opposite side of Rachel. "Did I?" He laughed when the girl pouted. "Well, I guess you'll both have to do it."

"I get to walk him first," Ruby said. Rachel immediately protested, and Grant shushed them both.

"Let's make a schedule," he said. "Ruby you can walk him on Mondays, Wednesdays, and Fridays. Rachel, you get Tuesdays, Thursdays, and Saturdays. I'll take him out on Sundays. Deal?"

The girls agreed, and Grant said, "Hey, girls, what's the name of your teacher this year?"

"Miss Turnsbell," Rachel said.

"And your principal?" Grant thought his voice sounded false and a bit too high. Megan would've noticed. She would've wanted to know why Grant needed to know the name of the principal. She would've hooked him with her eyes and discussed his question with Landon—and all the ranch wives—for weeks.

"Miss Sharpe," Ruby said.

"Do you know her first name?"

Ruby stared at him with a blank look in her eyes, and Grant chuckled. "I guess not. All right, it looks like your dad is ready to eat."

The girls ran toward the patio, and Grant shelved his sleuthing for the evening. He had a computer and the ranch had excellent WiFi. He could figure out the principal's name without bringing anyone else into it.

———

SHANNON SHARPE. *Shannon Sharpe. Shannon Sharpe.*

She'd certainly looked sharp, if Grant's memory could be trusted. He'd seen the woman around at town functions, always from a distance. Their circles had never overlapped, and though the website said she'd been principal for six years, he couldn't remember meeting her once.

He drove himself to church on Sunday morning, declining Emmett's usual offer. He hadn't had to provide an excuse either, something he appreciated about his friendship with the barrel horse trainer. No unnecessary questions. Your business was your business. Even his wife seemed to be that way, and Grant liked Molly a whole lot too.

But he wanted to be able to linger after church today, see if he could somehow come face-to-face with the blonde who'd confronted him on Friday. He could start with an apology, but he was also hoping to end with something else.

His heart seemed to twist with the road as he made his way down the canyon. He'd been going back to the elementary school to catch a glimpse of another woman. Another blonde, a second grade teacher there. He knew things between them wouldn't work out, and yet he'd had the hardest time letting Claire go.

He wasn't even sure why. Only that his soul felt called to the elementary school, and so he'd gone a few times.

A skin of embarrassment encased him as he remembered the spark in Shannon's eyes when she'd said he really needed to stop hanging around. He wondered how much she knew about him, and if she had a boyfriend, and if she liked cowboys.

Someone like her certainly didn't seem like the cowboy-loving type. No, he pictured her with a suit-wearing lawyer, or someone who owned their own ranch. Not someone who simply trained cattle to come out of the chute right and to trot off after they'd been roped and wrestled to the ground.

Still, Grant held his head high as he entered the church. He made a decent, honest living, and he shouldn't have to apologize for it. He'd chosen it after his retirement from the rodeo. He'd never topped the leaderboards the way Ted and Landon had. Never won multiple championships the way Justin and Walker had. But he'd made enough to live on, enough to invest, enough to support himself comfortably for a while—and then he'd blown it all.

He pushed the negative thoughts away, the way he'd learned to do in his therapy sessions, and stalled in the doorway of the chapel, his eyes scanning for those loose, blonde curls. Problem was, Brush Creek seemed to have a disproportionate number of blondes, most of whom Grant had taken out at least once. He seemed to have a new girl-friend every few weeks—at least until Claire.

When she'd broken up with him last fall, right after school started, Grant hadn't immediately gotten back on the dating wagon.

He suspected his thirtieth birthday had something to do with that, but he wasn't sure what. Just maybe that he now felt too old to be flirting with every female and "just having a good time."

He wanted that too. But he also now wanted to settle down. The feeling was as foreign as it was right, and he wasn't quite sure what to do about it. He did know that Miss Shannon Sharpe was the first woman in almost ten months who'd even remotely interested him, and he wasn't going to just ignore that.

Grant didn't see Shannon, and he wasn't sure he'd recognize her from the back even if he had. So he slipped down the aisle and sat on the end of a row by himself. Megan usually made sure he had someone to sit by, and Grant secretly believed she liked having Grant on the end of their bench so he could help entertain the kids. He didn't mind, and maybe Shannon would like that he was good with kids.

He shifted in his seat, very aware that he'd attended church for the past few years with Megan and Landon's family, and he'd never seen Shannon once. Why should today be any different? Simply because he'd seen her on Friday afternoon and liked her in-charge attitude? Her dangly earrings? Her soft curls?

He almost scoffed out loud. He was being so ridiculous. Clearing his throat, he focused on the front of the chapel and listened to the sermon. He didn't allow his gaze to wander, and he kept his attention on the preacher's words.

The meeting ended, and Grant didn't jump to his feet. He lingered the way he wanted to and scanned the people heading out. He didn't see Shannon and he reasoned that maybe she didn't go to church. Maybe she was sick today. So many maybes.

With the chapel almost empty, he finally stood and made his way up the aisle. The sun shone through the open doors, where Pastor Peters stood talking to patrons. Grant glanced down the hall, where a side door waited. He considered escaping that way, but he heard his name in Landon's voice.

He turned toward his boss, who was really so much more than that. Grant would do anything for Landon—including driving to Vernal at the drop of a hat to get an anniversary gift for Megan—because Landon had provided a refuge for Grant when he needed it most. He'd paid off Grant's gambling debts, given him a job, and provided a way for Grant to make amends and then make something of his life.

Grant was working on it, every day of his life. He almost had Landon paid back, and he loved the work he did on the ranch.

And here was Landon again, doing what Grant thought to be impossible. He gestured toward Grant, and Shannon glanced his way. Her face brightened, and she smiled. Her cheekbones became more prominent, and her beauty made Grant's heart tumble over a couple of beats.

"Grant," Landon said again. "This is Shannon Sharpe, the principal at Brush Creek Elementary. She's going to be...well, I'll let her explain it. I don't quite get it."

Shannon strode forward and extended her hand, her

teeth just as white as he remembered. Her makeup was flawless and not a single hair sat out of place. She wore a black pencil skirt with a pink blouse, a silver and black necklace that laid in the perfect places across her collarbone, and a pair of matching earrings.

"Nice to meet you, Grant," she said. She cast a quick glance at Landon. "As I was telling Mister Edmunds here, the superintendent of schools wants to do a summer riding program for our underprivileged kids. You know, the ones who qualify for summer school and free and reduced lunch."

Grant was having a hard time breathing and listening at the same time. Shannon smelled like floral lotion, and Grant wanted to find out what brand and buy a vat of it.

"Sure," he said, though he wasn't sure about much of anything at the moment.

"He mentioned Brush Creek Horse Farm, and we both thought it would be the best location for our students." She looked at Landon again. "You'll be compensated, and we won't have more than ten students up at the ranch at a time. We'll do all the transportation and everything." She switched her attention back to Grant. "We just need someone to help with the horseback riding lessons."

The way she gazed at him with such hope and self-assurance at the same time caused Grant's confidence to rise too. "I can give horseback riding lessons." He met Landon's eye. "Right?"

Landon studied him for a moment past normal. "How long would the riding lessons be?"

"We'll do our regular summer school classes in the morning," Shannon said. "And we'd like to bring kids up once a week. For them," she added quickly. "For you, it would be three groups of ten kids each day. From one o'clock to two-thirty. I'll come everyday, and I'll make sure I have teachers to supervise the children not doing riding lessons."

Everything she said sounded great, especially the bit about her coming up to the ranch every day. Grant deferred to Landon. "What do you think, boss?"

"Justin's done horseback riding lessons with kids before," Landon mused, his hand coming up to stroke his jaw.

Grant saw his opportunity to see Shannon every day slipping away. He took a quick step toward Landon. "I can do the lessons."

Landon met his eye, and Grant hoped he didn't look too desperate, but he felt it coursing through him with the force of river rapids.

"Maybe if you have three cowboys who could spare a half an hour, we could have three groups going at once and only have to come up for thirty minutes," Shannon said.

Landon blinked like he'd just realized that Shannon still stood there. "That would be great, if we have facilities to do horseback riding lessons for thirty kids at a time. Ten is going to be a challenge." He glanced around the lobby. "I don't even know if we have ten horses that can do riding lessons."

Grant could barely swallow. "I'm sure we can rustle them up."

Landon's eyebrows drew down, but Grant couldn't say anything right here, right now. He finally looked away from his boss, sighing and taking a few steps away. Not far enough so he couldn't hear Landon say, "Look, Miss Sharpe, we'll need a couple of days to look at our horses, and I'll need to figure out who I can spare."

"Does it have to be horseback riding lessons?" Grant asked, lunging back into the conversation, his mind racing.

Landon gave him an inquisitive look, but again, Grant felt like he couldn't say much.

"I'm just sayin' that maybe if she's bringing out thirty kids, that we could all do something with, I don't know, say five of them. Thirty minutes. They head back down the canyon, and we get back to work."

"What kind of something?" Landon asked.

Grant felt the weight of his boss's stare and Shannon's, and both were equally heavy. "I don't know," Grant said. "Roping, maybe. Horse care. Heck, they can sweep barns."

"Well." Shannon chuckled as she shouldered her way into the conversation. "We want this to be something fun for the kids. Otherwise, we'll just send them back to daycare." Her blue eyes were like sapphires and Grant had to blink and look away before he became mesmerized.

"I need a few days," Landon said. "Can I call you if I have more questions?"

"Of course." She pulled out her phone and checked it. "Would you like my number?"

"I can just call—"

"I'll take it," Grant said, interrupting Landon with too much eagerness in his tone. He noticed the way Landon settled his weight away from Grant and nodded. He knew of Grant's interest, but somehow Grant didn't care. He wanted Shannon Sharpe's phone number, and if he had to use his job at the ranch to get it, he'd do it.

"I'm sure we can work somethin' out," Grant said with a grin. "I'll let you know, all right, Miss Sharpe?"

She grinned up at Grant with a flirty glint in her eye, spun on her bedazzled heels, and walked out of the church.

"Oh, boy," Landon said. "You sweet on her?"

Grant scoffed. "Sweet, no." He turned back to his friend. "Interested, yes."

Landon chuckled. "Well, the whole town knows that now."

"Whatever," Grant said. "There were like, two people left when she *offered* her phone number." His phone felt like a delicious prize, and he flipped it over in his palm, wondering how long he should wait to call Shannon. Probably at least more than five minutes.

Landon clapped Grant on the shoulder and leaned in close. "She seems like more than even you can handle. Probably should be careful."

"Yeah," Grant said, giddy and trying not to show it.

"And we'll have to talk about the program," he said as he started toward the exit. "Something like that doesn't just magically happen, you know."

"I know," Grant called after him, grateful once again for Landon Edmunds.

CHAPTER 3

Shannon didn't hear from Landon—or Grant—on Monday. Or Tuesday. Or Wednesday. By Thursday, she'd bitten all her fingernails down to the point of painful, and she had an appointment with her supervisor that afternoon. She'd hoped to have some news for him, maybe a checklist of items she needed, or some questions from the ranchers up the canyon.

Instead, she had bupkis. She didn't have Grant's number, but she'd managed to find a woefully outdated website for the horse ranch, which included a contact number. She called that, surprised when a woman answered.

"Oh, hello," Shannon said. "I'm looking for Landon Edmunds? Or maybe Grant...Something." She trilled out a laugh that sounded fake and drummed her nailless fingers on her desk.

"Ford," the woman said.

"I'm sorry?"

"Grant's last name is Ford. But Landon is standing

right here." The phone switched hands, and Landon said, "Hello?" in a somewhat grumpy tone, if Shannon could read the inflection in his voice.

"Landon," she said. "It's Shannon Sharpe from the school. I have a meeting with my boss today, and I'm just wondering if you've had enough time—and have enough information—to make a decision on the summer riding program."

He exhaled, which might as well have been a "No, I haven't given it a second thought."

"I—Can I send someone down to talk to you this morning?" he said instead.

"Sure, of course."

"Great, I'll get Grant down there before lunch."

She accepted his offer and hung up. She smoothed her blouse and combed her fingers through her hair, though the man hadn't even left the ranch yet. She shouldn't even be thinking about him past a contact on the ranch. Just because he was handsome didn't mean they were a match.

But you could be, she thought. And therein sat the real opportunity, the real reason her heart jumped from one side of her chest to the other whenever she thought about Grant filling her office doorway.

An hour later, he did just that. She glanced away from her computer and nearly gasped. Her face relaxed into a smile and she forgot about next year's budget, which she was trying to align with the needs of the school and students.

"Hey," she said.

"Hey, yourself." Grant returned her grin and stepped into the office.

Though it was large, and she had three chairs around a table in front of her desk, he filled all the available space with his charisma and charm. So much so that Shannon leaned forward on her elbows as she said, "Have a seat."

He sat and said, "Landon said you needed to see me."

She pulled a folder toward her. "Yes, I'm meeting with my supervisor this afternoon, and I need to be able to tell him something." She shuffled some papers around, looking for the one she needed.

"Landon says we can't do ten kids at a time," Grant said. "So I don't know if you can make something else work, but we don't have the horses or manpower for that."

She looked up at him, unable to find the list of confirmed summer school students. "I overestimated how many students we'd have enrolled in the program. It will be less than what I said originally."

He swiped his dark brown cowboy hat off his head to reveal a headful of delicious black hair. "I'm not sure what you know about Brush Creek Horse Ranch, but we don't breed horses. We train them into rodeo champions."

Shannon blinked, because no, she hadn't truly known what the horse ranch did. Dr. Vincent had suggested some outdoor activities for the low-income students, and Shannon had blurted out horseback riding lessons.

"How many horses do you have?"

"That can do horseback riding lessons?" Grant replaced his hat and peered at her from under its brim. "Probably three or four. And they're not ranch horses. They're our own personal horses. Like I could use Gwyneth Paltrow for a lesson, but—"

Shannon burst into laughter. "Wait a second. Gwyneth Paltrow?"

Grant's stare had level ten intensity in it. "She's my horse."

Shannon cocked her head and tried to find the reason behind the name. Amusement sparked in his eyes, and she ended up lifting both hands in acquiescence. "So no horse-back riding." Her delight over his horse's name faded as the possibility of spending some time with him disappeared on the horizon.

"I don't think so." He looked genuinely sorry, and she could barely stomach the dark, puppy-dog eyes.

"So I'll come up with something else." She sighed and closed the folder, all her questions and checklists useless if she couldn't even get five kids up to the ranch.

"How many kids do you have in your program?"

"Total? Or my low-income group?"

"Either."

"I have about a hundred coming for summer school. Maybe twenty or so of those we'd like to keep for an extended experience in June."

"Just June?"

"Yes, summer school is just in June."

Grant looked over her left shoulder, the cogs clearly working in his head. "Even if we split them into five groups, that's still four kids." He met her eye. "Maybe I can bring a horse down to them."

"What do you mean?"

"I can bring Gwyneth down here. Give some lessons in horse care. Let the kids ride her. They wouldn't *learn* to ride, but I could lead them."

"All right. That sounds like one week—tops—of afternoons."

"We could take them to the swimming hole out by the strawberry fields," Grant suggested. "I could ask the bakery if they could do a couple of lessons on making bread or cookies. Something like that. I know the guy who runs the parks department, and maybe he'd take the kids out into the wooded area at Oxbow Park."

"We did just want to give the kids some outdoor experiences they might not otherwise be able to do...." Shannon mused. "I'll talk to my supervisor this afternoon." She stood, though she wanted the meeting to last a bit longer. "I'll let you know if we need you and Gwyneth." She beamed at him and reached across the desk to shake his hand.

"So I can't help?"

Shannon blinked at him. "You want to help...how?"

He shrugged. "Maybe I could be in charge of your extended programs."

"I have teachers for that," she said, immediately regretting it.

"Of course." Grant ducked his head and hightailed it out of the office. Just like that afternoon she'd told him he had to leave, he didn't look back.

She sank into her chair, her mind racing. Had she just done it again? Told him to leave? Frantic, she returned to her budget. Could she afford to hire a summer extended program director?

She ran through the faculty she needed for the morning classes, and calculated the number of students who'd stay for lunch and then the extended afternoon session. She could do the lunchtime recess...and employ Grant to plan and carry out the afternoon activities.

If she limited the program to twenty students, she and Grant could handle the hour and half by themselves.

She leaned back in her chair. And she'd get to see him everyday like she'd hoped. A smile flirted with her mouth, and she quelled it. It all looked good on paper, but she'd have to tell the faculty the summer school positions were only half-time—which most of them already were anyway—and Grant would have to go through the hiring process at the school district.

Which meant she needed to get him started on that right away.

She leapt from her desk, wondering how many minutes had gone by since he'd left. She glanced out her window, which faced the front parking lot and saw the flash of a red truck as it pulled out of a stall and eased onto the road.

That had to be him. Her heart fell, but it rebounded quickly, and she lifted the phone again.

———

HALF AN HOUR LATER, she sat in the nearly empty diner, the mid-morning crowd limited to a couple of elderly gentlemen and a single waitress.

Grant finally pushed through the door, making the bells jingle, and swept the diner before heading her direction. He slid into the booth across from her and glared. "All right," he said. "I'm here."

She pushed a folder across the table to him and lifted her lukewarm coffee to her lips. "I'll need you to fill out the paperwork for the district if you want to be my summer extended program director."

He blinked and didn't make a move for the folder. "What now?"

"I ran some numbers, and I can afford to hire you if you want the job." She sipped the coffee again. "Of course, I have to officially list the job, and technically I have to interview for the position, but, well, you'll come down for an interview, right?"

"I suppose so."

"We'll have to plan the program together. I can't afford another advisor, so you and I alone will run the program."

Grant leaned forward. "Is that so?"

Shannon recognized flirting when she saw it, and she suppressed her smile behind her coffee mug. "Totally so."

He flipped open the folder and looked at the top page. "I have to do all this to apply for the job?"

"The school district is very thorough."

"Fingerprints, wow."

"We require them for parents coming on field trips too." She shrugged. "You're working with kids."

He closed the folder. "I'll get it done." Grant swallowed and slid to the end of the booth as if he was going to leave already. "Hey, Shannon—uh, Miss Sharpe? Is there a policy about co-workers, um, bosses and employees, maybe, you know, dating?"

Shannon stared at him, at a loss for words for maybe the first time.

"I'll look it up," Grant said, grinning. He left her sitting there, even more attracted to him that he'd made the first move.

CHAPTER 4

Grant whistled as he went about his work, his thoughts revolving around the pretty blonde he'd met with that morning. He couldn't believe she'd called Megan and asked for his number. Couldn't believe Megan had given it to her. Couldn't believe Shannon wanted him to be the elementary school's summer program director.

At the same time, he thought it sounded like fun. He'd always liked kids—and he definitely wanted to get to know Shannon better. Right now, she pretty much scared him to death. The way she had every hair in place, jewels sparkling on her fingers, and all her rough edges polished.

Grant wondered how he could carry on a conversation with someone as sophisticated as her, and his stomach tightened. What would she think of his past failures? For sure she had never failed at anything. No, she was the type of woman who put her mind to something and made it happen.

Grant finished cleaning out the calf pens and headed

outside. His phone rang, and he hoped for half a second that it would be Shannon.

But it was his sister, Jordan. At least it wasn't Meredith. Both of his sisters lived in San Antonio, only miles from where they all grew up. They were both married, with several kids between them, and Grant was the baby brother—the black sheep—who'd broken ranks.

He thought briefly about telling her about Shannon, but decided against it. He swiped the call to voicemail and continued into the horse barn. He saddled Gwyneth and led her across the lane and into his yard. He threw the reins around a tree branch and went inside to get Bullseye.

He needed some time out in the open, away from the ranch, in order to find his center again. Everything had been thrown off since Friday when he'd come face-to-face with Shannon.

The bulldog jogged ahead of him and down the road while Grant swung himself onto Gwyneth's back. He let the horse plod along, not pushing her toward any goal. She'd get him to the stream without any direction from him. Horses always did.

He let the sky swallow him and all his thoughts. He even forgot about Jordan until she called again.

"Hey Jordan," he said. Maybe she just had something funny to say about their dad, who was getting kookier by the month.

"Grant," she said. "Mom's wondering if you'll be coming home for the fireworks this year."

Grant didn't even bother to smother his groan. His mom couldn't seem to figure out that there were fireworks all over the country on Independence Day.

"Oh, come on," Jordan said. "You haven't been home in three years for our family get-together."

"I come at other times of the year," he said. "Summer is really hard for me." Going home at all was hard for him. He loved his nieces and nephews, but sometimes seeing his sisters and their families reminded him acutely of what he didn't have.

And his mom asked so many questions, Grant always feared he'd end up slipping about his gambling problem. He hadn't put any bets on games in years—since he'd come to Brush Creek—but the temptation was still there, ever-present.

He exhaled, wishing the sky could swallow this weak part of himself too.

"Just think about it," Jordan said.

"Well, I'm running a summer school program this year, so I highly doubt I'll have the time off," he said.

"A summer school program?" The level of interest in Jordan's voice sounded heavily in Grant's ears.

"I mean, I don't have the job yet. It's just something I've been discussing with the principal."

"What does he want you to do?"

Grant didn't correct her incorrect pronoun and launched into the general concept of the program. By the time he hung up with his sister, Grant was eager to get home and get started on all those papers.

——————

THE JOB HAS BEEN POSTED.

Grant saw Shannon's text as he walked from the cattle

chutes to the homestead for lunch the following week. She'd texted a lot over the past several days, and Grant had enjoyed their flirtatious banter, even if it wasn't in person.

Every time he saw her name on the screen, he smiled. Every time she mentioned the job, his heart pumped harder. Every time she asked about Gwyneth and how he'd named his horse, he'd responded with *None of your business*.

He didn't want to tell her that he'd always had a thing for blondes, and Gwyneth Paltrow was his favorite actress. He didn't want to tell her about a lot of things, but the horse seemed to be at the forefront most days.

So I apply on the website?

Yes, please. Soon. I can interview as soon as someone applies.

I'll do it right now. He bypassed the homestead, where everyone usually gathered on the front patio for lunch, and headed for his cabin across the lane.

Unfortunately, the school district's website was less than user-friendly, and it took most of Grant's lunch hour to get his application in. He fired off a quick *It's done* as he hurried back across the street and into the horse barn, where he was slated to work with Justin that afternoon. He had a horse that was only a week or two away from being ready, and he needed all the practice he could get with cattle running from chutes and cowboys riding and roping from his back.

Grant moved down the aisle in the horse barn, stopping at each horse though he was already a bit late. The horses spoke to his soul the same way the soothing words of Pastor Peters did. Though they didn't say anything in English, their calm spirits spoke to his.

He stopped outside the stall of one of Emmett's horses, a tall, proud Friesian that had recently been bought by a cowgirl out of Montana. Emmett had been seen brooding around the barn, bathing Double Chocolate Latte and taking him out for rides in the evenings.

Grant understood the emotional connection between a cowboy and his horse, and he wasn't sure how the other guys could work with a horse for so long and then sell it, let it go.

"You gonna win some championships?" Grant asked the horse, who looked proud and regal. "I bet you are."

His phone buzzed and Shannon had said *When can you come for an interview?*

Grant honestly didn't know. Landon kept a calendar in the office in the arena, but Grant lived it day by day. He knew what training his calves needed, and he worked with them every morning. His afternoons were spent working with horses, or cleaning out stalls, or helping with other ranch tasks. It was the only way he'd been able to convince Landon that he could be the summer program director and keep up with his work on the ranch.

"I'll put in whatever hours it takes," Grant had said. "Don't reduce my tasks. I'll work well into the evening."

Because Landon had known of Grant's interest in Shannon, he'd given his permission for Grant to apply for the job.

Not sure. Need to check the calendar.

Let me know.

Grant turned as if he'd go check right now, but Justin called "Grant, let's go," from behind him, and Grant had no choice but to go.

———

The next day, Grant pulled up to the elementary school again, the sight of it almost as soothing as walking through the horse barn. He entered the office and glanced at the secretary sitting there.

"Is Miss Sharpe in her office?"

"I'll page her. She had something happen in the gym." She picked up her phone and sent a message, adding, "You can go sit down, if you like."

He tipped his hat and entered the office, the scent of Shannon overwhelming him and she wasn't even present. He took a deep drag of the powdery-lotiony scent, moved behind the desk, and claimed her chair. He sighed as he stretched his arms above his head and looked out the wall of windows behind her desk.

He wondered if she ever took the time to enjoy the view from this chair, or if her tasks as the principal kept her running from dawn until dusk. He wondered if her life simply couldn't mesh with his. After all, she was in-charge, powerful, educated, flitting from important task to important task.

Grant's life was much simpler. He knew it, and he enjoyed it. Could Shannon ever understand that kind of life? Did she even want to?

"It's premature anyway," he said to himself, swinging around in the chair to find Shannon leaning one hip into the doorway, her arms folded across her chest, a grin the size of the Rocky Mountains on her face.

"What's premature?" she asked, stepping into the office and closing the door behind her.

CHAPTER 5

Shannon sat on the other side of the desk—a whole new view for her. And she liked the view sitting in front of her. Grant leaned onto the desk, a ruddiness entering his face and making his black sideburns stand out.

"Nothing," he said quickly. "Now, I heard you were down in the lunchroom. Throwing food again?" He wagged his finger at her like she was a naughty child. "We don't do that here, you know."

She burst into laughter. When she quieted, she said, "That's what you think I do, isn't it?"

A blank look crossed his face. "This isn't what you do? Reprimand naughty children?"

"Not even close." She thought of the budget reports, the supply money she needed, the first grade teacher who cried at the drop of a hat, the sixth grade teacher who couldn't get along with her co-teacher, and the IEPs she had scheduled. Not to mention the scheduling for next year, the faculty meeting she'd be running tomorrow, the fact that the secretary was leaving at the end of the year, and that her whole fourth grade team was in open rebellion against the newly adopted math curriculum.

He grinned and stood. "Well, I really have no idea what you do, but one of those things is interviews, so we should probably do that." He came around the desk and Shannon met him in the narrow walkway between the wall.

She paused and looked up at him, the charge between them very real and very hot. Surely he had to feel it too. Boldly, she touched his hand, squeezed his fingers, and continued past him. Heat rushed to her face now, and surely she looked like a cooked lobster with a blonde wig by the time she sat behind her desk and faced him again.

"This is more of a formality than anything," she said. "But I'd love to ask you some questions." The devilish side of her had all kinds of questions. Personal questions.

He swallowed, and guards flew into place in his expression. "Go ahead."

"Past work experience?"

"I've been a cowboy on the ranch for three years," he said. "Up there, I help with the farming, and I train the cattle that we then sell to the rodeo. They have to be trained how to come out of the chute, where to run, that kind of stuff."

"Mm hm." She didn't look away from him. He had a strong jaw, and straight white teeth. Along with his full lips, Shannon found him downright attractive.

"Before that, I was—" He cleared his throat. "I wandered a bit after I quit the rodeo, which I did for about eight years."

"Wandered? That sounds interesting."

"It wasn't that interesting." He shifted in his seat, and for someone who spent all her time analyzing whether a young human was lying to her or not, she sensed something.

"You didn't work during that time?" she asked.

"Didn't need to."

"But you do now?"

"Money runs out, and I wasn't a champion."

"No?"

He shook his head and pressed those lips into a line. She focused there, her thoughts only on kissing him. She yanked herself back to her job, her office, this interview.

"I mean, I won here and there. I made enough to support myself and to live for a year. Now I work at Brush Creek."

She glanced down at the official paperwork she'd had her secretary compile. She had to make this look legit, after all. She'd read through it. She knew how old Grant was, that his birthday was coming up in September, even his middle name.

"Do you have a girlfriend?" she asked.

Grant's smile was instant and that tether between them pulled. "How is that related to the summer program?"

"Oh, it's not." Shannon smiled and picked up a pen. "I just want to know."

"Do you have a boyfriend?" he asked.

"Not at the moment." She loved this flirtatious banter, liked that Grant didn't take everything so seriously. All the men she'd been dating for the past couple of years were so proud of themselves, so into their careers.

"I was just wondering if Gwyneth is going to be a problem." Shannon ducked her head and looked at Grant through her eyelashes.

He chuckled. "Why don't you just ask what you want to ask?"

She lifted her chin. "All right then. Why did you name your horse Gwyneth Paltrow?"

He folded his arms. "I like blondes."

Heat writhed through her bloodstream. "Are you still interested in Claire?" Shannon hadn't said anything to her second grade teacher about Grant hanging around, but she should probably mention it if she was going to start dating Grant. And she wanted to start dating Grant. Maybe he was free this weekend.

Grant blinked furiously. "Claire?"

"She teaches second grade here? You dated her last fall."

"Summer," he corrected. "And no, I'm not interested in her."

"Summer fling?"

"For her, apparently." He glared back at her, most of the fun gone from the conversation.

"Just one more question then," Shannon said.

"Shoot."

"Are you free for dinner on Friday night?"

LATER THAT EVENING, Shannon completed the hiring paperwork for Grant and clicked all the right buttons on the back end of the system to get the job filled. She leaned away from her computer desk in her office, one long sigh accompanying the movement.

Her shoulders ached, and her head pounded. She glanced at her phone, the screen as dark as her mood. Hannah hadn't responded to her message. Shannon had known she wouldn't. Still, she couldn't help sending the text, and she'd almost called.

She wasn't sure why. It wasn't her sister's birthday. Maybe because the little blonde girl she'd seen skipping to the bus earlier that afternoon had reminded her so strongly of Hannah that Shannon couldn't stop thinking about her.

They used to talk everyday, even if it was just a simple one-line text. Sometimes their conversations would last for a couple of hours in the evening while Shannon made dinner and tidied up the house.

Steve had ruined everything, and a loathing so strong Shannon couldn't contain it surged through her body. Shannon had been so excited for her younger sister. Finally, one of the girls was going to get married. She'd never seen Hannah so happy, could actually hear the pure joy in her voice whenever they spoke.

Their conversations had turned to wedding planning, and Shannon hadn't minded at all. She hadn't spent much time fantasizing about her big day, but Hannah had. She had an idea for what she wanted the dress to look like, and where the ceremony would be held, and the exact shade of pink she wanted for the roses in her bouquet.

She'd been planning a spring wedding, one that would've happened about a month ago if Steve hadn't revealed who he truly was. Of course, he'd only done that to Shannon and it seemed no one believed her.

She picked up her phone and dialed her mother, realizing too late what time it was. She hung up hastily so she didn't wake her mom, who was known to go to bed before eight o'clock. She felt unsettled inside, and she wasn't even sure why. Sometimes she craved silence, but now wasn't one of those times.

She opened her browser and turned on an Internet radio station, a measure of relief pushing away some of her disquiet as the sound filtered through the room.

The silence in her soul continued for a couple more days, despite her being surrounded by people and busier than ever at work. The end of the year was always a little insane, but this year felt especially so.

By the time Grant pulled into her driveway on Friday evening, she was ready for some noise. She answered the door completely ready to go but still said, "Come in," anyway.

He ducked through the doorway wearing a pair of jeans and a black polo that made him seem dark and dangerous. He swiped his hat off his head, and she realized the hat was black tonight. Everything about him was a shade of midnight, and she stepped into him and slid her fingers up his arm. "It's good to see you." Fire raced from her fingertips to her elbow to her shoulder, and she shivered.

Grant inhaled and took her hand in his. "You seem tired."

"Not what a woman wants to hear." She smiled and gripped his fingers a little tighter.

"I didn't say you *looked* tired." He glanced around her house, and she wondered what he saw. "I imagine the end of the school year is tough."

"I definitely can't wait until June." She lifted her purse

from the end table. "And I'm completely ready for dinner. I think you mentioned burgers in your text this morning."

"You eat burgers?"

"With everything on them."

"Well, let's go then."

She held his hand to his truck, let him open the door for her, and sat right next to him on the bench seat as he drove. He told her about his family in San Antonio and his two married sisters. Shannon didn't volunteer any information about her family, and thankfully, Grant didn't ask.

He drove back toward Vernal, bypassing the town where Shannon usually went on dates. Another ten minutes down the road, they came to a tiny hole-in-the-wall town called Clawson. He turned right, and then took another right farther down the road.

"This feels sketchy," she said with a somewhat nervous chuckle. "There is a restaurant out here, right?"

"I wouldn't call it a restaurant," he said. "That's much too generous. But they do have delicious burgers."

Up ahead, on the left, a single sign poked into the air. It simply read Dave's and three trucks were parked out front. "At least we're driving the right vehicle," she said, employing her principal eagle eyes to scan the place. For what, she wasn't sure, but a trickle of fear tripped through her. She liked it.

"I should've worn different shoes," she said as he pulled into the dirt and parked. She glanced at her heels and then Grant.

"Nah," he said. "Those are fine." He got out of the truck and turned back to her. "More than fine. I like 'em." He grinned at her as she slid across the bench and let him help her down. He didn't step back and she was suddenly glad for the increased height the black heels gave her. She gazed at him, noticing the storm in his eyes, and gripped his elbows in her hands.

"Let's eat," he said, clearing his throat as he put some distance between them. She captured his hand and tread carefully on the somewhat rutted surface that led to the establishment.

One step inside, and Shannon knew she was going to have a great night. Only six tables filled the space, with a bar in the back. Near that sat a one-man stage with a karaoke machine. Two of the tables were occupied, and several stools at the bar. No one was singing, but music played from the ancient jukebox near where they'd entered.

"Grant." A man came around the bar and pulled Grant into a big old man-hug, complete with the back-slapping and everything. "What the heck are you doin' here? I haven't seen you since you was with that—" His eyes cut to Shannon and back to Grant. "Well, for a long time. You guys eatin' tonight?"

"Yeah." Grant freed himself from the other man and gestured to him. "Shannon, this is Dave."

"*The* Dave?"

"The one and only." He bowed slightly at the waist and shook her hand. "You two datin'?"

Her eyes flew to Grant's and held. He shrugged. "Maybe. This is our first date."

Warmth oozed through her like honey, and she tucked her arm into Grant's. "How do you know Grant?" she asked.

"We're, uh, old rodeo pals." Dave turned and pointed to

the table farthest from the stage and the bar. "Y'all can sit there. I'll get Tiffany to bring you some menus."

Shannon went with Grant to the indicated table and sat, her jeans a bit tighter than she liked. Maybe it was all the stress eating she'd been doing. "This place has menus?"

"Don't get excited," Grant said. "You'll see."

Tiffany appeared carrying two slips of paper that looked like Dave had scratched out the choices by hand. In blue pen. "Special tonight is the all-American bacon burger."

Grant looked at her, eyebrows raised. She nodded and said, "We'll take two of those. And I want Diet Coke." When she looked back at Grant, he wore a disgruntled look. "What?"

"Nothing." He handed back the "menu." "I'll take regular Coke."

Shannon watched the waitress go, her emotions teeming in her stomach. She'd gone and been all take-charge. She knew—she knew—her ordering for both of them had bothered Grant. Why did she do things like that? And better yet, how did she get herself to stop?

"I'm sorry," she said to break the awkward silence that had fallen between them.

"For what?"

"Ordering for us like I'm...I don't even know what." She waved in the direction the waitress had gone, not quite sure how to articulate what she was feeling. All she knew was she didn't like the squirrelly way her nerves were firing.

"You're used to being in charge." It wasn't a question.

"I don't have to be," she said.

He leaned closer, something between a playful smirk

and an annoyed grimace on his face. "I'll admit, I like a woman who knows how to be in charge."

She stared at him, sure she'd heard him wrong. Most men found her intimidating, and once, a man had broken up with her because she "terrified him."

"Okay," she said.

"But we're not at work or school tonight. So maybe I can take care of you a little?"

She liked the sound of that, and she relaxed. "Yeah, okay."

"Good." He reached across the table and covered both of her hands with one of his. "So, tell me about your family."

CHAPTER 6

Grant liked listening to Shannon talk. She had obviously been raised in a small town, and he guessed her parents still lived there. He had to guess, because she'd only said one sentence about her family before deviating into another topic.

The words started to blur together as he thought about how polished and sophisticated she was. She'd ordered for both of them, and she'd initiated almost all of their physical contact. While on some level he liked that, on another, it was completely intimidating. Again, he wondered how someone as put together as Shannon could like a simple cowboy like him.

But she seemed to, and Grant was no stranger to dating. He'd felt the chemistry between them, and it was nearly explosive. Their drinks came and he unwrapped his straw carefully before downing half his soda. He needed to cool off, get his head back in the conversation, and find out if he really liked Shannon underneath all the makeup, jewelry, and confidence.

He'd met a lot of cowboys and cowgirls like her, and every single one of them struggled with something. He theorized what her weakness would be, and he hoped he'd be around to help her with it.

She finished a story about a third grader who brought live chickens to school, and their food arrived. Grant tried to soothe his frayed emotions with beef and bacon and a toasted bun. It didn't quite work, and he couldn't quite put his finger on what was bothering him.

Shannon was gorgeous, educated, and interested. She was interesting.

Finally, he realized that maybe she was a little too perfect. And that sooner or later, she'd realize how much better she was than him, and that they didn't even exist on the same planet in the dating universe.

But she laughed with him, and snuggled close on the drive home, and invited him to sip coffee on her back patio, all of which he enjoyed. His thoughts revolved around kissing her, and as his exhaustion increased, he finally stood and said, "Well, I have to work tomorrow."

"Do you work every weekend?"

"Sure do. The animals need to be fed everyday." He pulled her to her feet too and played with her fingers. "This was fun, right?"

"I had a great time." She beamed up at him, and he leaned down.

Her eyes drifted closed and Grant could kiss her right now if he wanted to. And he definitely wanted to.

"No kissing on the first date," he whispered in her ear, completely bypassing her lips. "Didn't your mama teach you that?"

"What?" she asked breathlessly.

Grant held her in his arms, a giddiness in his system he didn't quite understand. "Never trust a man who kisses on the first date. So." He stepped back and exhaled all his desires. "I'll see you later."

She followed him through the house and leaned into the open front door while he stepped onto the porch. "When?" she asked.

"How about you come up to the ranch tomorrow?" he asked, wondering if he'd just signed his own death warrant. "You want to take the kids to do some outdoor stuff. Maybe we could get you ready for that."

The briefest flash of fear crossed her features before she smiled. "All right. What time?"

"After noon. I work with the cattle until lunchtime. My afternoons are much more relaxed."

"So about one?"

"Sure, one works." He tipped his hat and got himself down the steps and into his truck before he broke his rule about no kissing on the first date.

———

SHANNON DROVE A TINY LITTLE CAR, the first thing that made her stick out on the ranch. Grant had told her to come to his cabin, and the sporty silver number seemed completely out of place. He set his guitar down, resting it against the cabin, and stood. "Be nice," he told Bullseye, who stood at attention on the edge of the porch.

She unfolded herself from the car, and just like last night, she wore a tight pair of jeans that accentuated all her curves. Today she'd matched those with a yellow and white checkered shirt, knotted on the side so it fit her like a glove.

She'd traded the heels for a pair of sandals that looked like they were made of yellow string. He laughed as she approached. "What?" she asked as Bullseye sniffed her legs. She bent down and scrubbed him behind the ears and patted his ribs. He gave her the stamp of approval, and Grant was impressed.

"You realize we're going to be outside." He glanced pointedly at her shoes. "Hiking, riding horses, you know. Cowboy stuff."

"You didn't specify what we'd be doing."

"I said we'd be doing some outdoor stuff like what we'd want the kids to do. Would you let them wear rubber bands for shoes?"

"These are not rubber bands."

Grant chuckled and slipped one arm around her waist, drawing her closer. At least she'd let him touch her first this time. *Probably because she's upset about the shoe teasing.*

He grinned down at her anyway. "You're not wearing any jewelry."

"I needed a day off," she said. "I didn't know you noticed my jewelry."

Grant swallowed and covered his nerves with a smile. "Oh, I noticed." He'd noticed everything about her, from the immaculate condition of her makeup to her somewhat chewed fingernails. He leaned closer. "You're kinda hard *not* to notice."

"I've noticed that you own at least two cowboy hats."

"At least being the operative words there," he said. "I

won't even tell you how many I have. Don't want you to think I have a fetish or something."

She tipped her head back and laughed, revealing a creamy throat Grant wanted to taste. He released her and stepped back, trying to infuse some reason into his head. He'd known Shannon for three weeks at best. Flirty texts, an upcoming summer working together, and one date didn't mean they were serious. But if he kissed her…. Well, in Grant's book, that was taking a relationship all the way to serious with a capital S.

"You should see my shoe racks," she said. "But I can quit any time I want."

Grant scoffed and then laughed as he led her down the front steps, Bullseye not about to miss out on the afternoon's adventure. "Sure you can. Let's go get the horses."

"Whoa. Horses? Plural?"

"Trust me, you don't wanna walk out to the trailhead. There's barely a path."

"I've never ridden a horse before. I thought…maybe I thought I could ride with you."

Grant cast her a sideways look and found open worry on her face. It actually soothed him, as did the atrocious footwear. They proved she was human, imperfect, and maybe a little quirky.

"I'll talk to Gwyneth." He bumped her with his hip and increased his pace when she protested, getting several paces ahead of her.

"I knew she was going to be a problem!" Shannon called after him, and Grant sent his laughter into the sky.

"All right," Grant said once they'd entered the barn. "I asked Landon if you could ride Crossfire, and I think you'll like him. He's about a hundred years old, so he's nice and gentle." He stopped outside the first horse stall, where Landon's personal horse lived. A beautiful brown and white horse, Crossfire was a thoroughbred. "He's an excellent first horse to ride."

Shannon's eyes widened as she gazed up at the horse. "He's so big."

"He has no bite," Grant said. "C'mon, I'll help you get his saddle."

"You're going to have to do it all," she said. "I've never ridden a horse before."

"And you grew up in Tennessee?"

"Kentucky."

"Even horsier."

"Horsier? Is that a word?"

He kicked a grin at her, glad she stood real close to him. "Sure it is."

"Where's Gwyneth? We need to have a little girl-to-girl talk." She scanned the stalls lining both sides of the aisle running down the middle of the barn.

Grant crossed to the other side and stepped down three stalls. His beautiful black horse met him at the gate, and his smile softened into one filled with love for the animal. "Hey, girl," he murmured to her. She flicked her tail and let her eyes close halfway. "I brought a friend to meet you. Told you we were goin' ridin' today." He moved sideways and let Shannon come closer.

"Well, this is about as non-blonde as you can get."

Grant slid one arm around her waist and drew Shannon into his side. "I didn't say *she* was blonde. I said I liked blondes."

Shannon switched her gaze from the horse's face to Grant's. "How many blondes have you dated?"

"A fair few."

"How many brunettes?"

"Some of them too."

"So you date a lot."

"I'd say so, yeah." He looked into her eyes. "Is that a problem?"

"Maybe for Gwyneth." She giggled at her own joke, and Grant tugged her tighter against him, an infectious smile crossing his lips too. He enjoyed the quiet moment with his horse and Shannon, who he hoped he could call his girl-friend. His muscles squeezed and tightened before they released quickly.

"So...are we dating?" he asked.

Shannon blinked, her giggles subsiding into something more serious. "You're the one who said our dinner last night was our first date." She tucked a curl behind her ear. "And you wouldn't kiss me, because you said it was the first date."

"So we must be." He focused on the horse again, warmth blooming beneath his breastbone. "That's good to know." He pushed out a breath and said, "Let's get ready to ride."

A good twenty minutes later, he finally had both horses saddled, in the yard, and Shannon ready to get on. She'd been pacing for the past ten minutes, working herself up to mounting the horse. Bullseye had flopped himself into the shade, and Grant wasn't sure he'd come now. He wasn't much for exercising or exploring.

"The horse isn't even gonna move," Grant assured her

again. "I'll help you." He couldn't stop smiling, because he liked every darn thing about this woman. He liked her anxiety. Liked her skinny jeans. Liked her nervous laughter.

And when she put her hand in his, he liked that too. "Foot there." He indicated the stirrup. "Other leg over." Shannon clearly worked out, because she had the leg and core strength to launch herself onto the horse.

Grant did the same, and he took her reins and looped them around Gwyneth's saddle horn. "All right. Now Crossfire's biggest weakness is he doesn't like water, and we'll be crossing a stream. So I'll lead—"

"Wait a minute. We're going into water?" She began fanning herself like she'd faint at any moment.

"The snow's barely started to melt. It's more of a trickle." He hoped. He hadn't actually been out to the stream yet, but it didn't get very full before June. "You'll see."

He whistled to Bullseye, who did join them, and set out, passing the homestead on his right and leaving behind Cabin Row on his left. They followed a dirt road for a few minutes and then he veered Gwyneth down a foot trail that wound like a ribbon through the wild grasses. The fields on either side of them had been recently ploughed in preparation for planting, and the dirt there would be loose and unforgiving.

A slight breeze tried to lift his cowboy hat from his head, and Grant pressed it further onto his head. He sighed in pure contentment. There was nothing he loved more than this land. He could feel God out here, and when he needed answers to problems, he never had to look farther than his own backyard.

"It's quiet out here," Shannon said, her voice shushed.

"It's great, isn't it?"

"Gives me a lot of room to think."

"That's what I like about it."

They didn't speak again until they came to the stream. Bullseye waded right in and the water was shallow enough that he didn't have to swim. Grant watched the bulldog with a measure of admiration and affection. The animal turned back when he reached the other side, his tongue lolling out of his smiling mouth, and Grant grinned at him before turning back to the horses.

"All right, Crossfire. Your turn," Grant said. "Nice and easy, bud. Come with Gwenny."

Shannon scoffed, and Grant grinned at her. Crossfire balked, and Grant tugged until the horse finally obeyed and sloshed into the water. "See? Easy."

"Oh!" Shannon yelped, and Grant swung around to look at her.

"What?"

"That water is *cold*."

"It's snow-melt runoff," he said. "So yeah. It's cold." He chuckled. "Did I not mention that?"

"You did *not* mention that." She gave him a disgruntled look, but all it did was get Grant's blood moving faster. He brought Crossfire even with Gwyneth and reached across the space between him and Shannon to hold her hand.

"The trailhead's another ten minutes or so, but you're not really wearing appropriate hiking shoes. Want to just relax here?"

She glanced around. "Where?"

"Here." He squeezed her hand and swung off his horse. "There are some trees down there, and we can let the horses graze in the pasture right behind that." He pointed about a hundred yards down the stream.

He led the horses—Crossfire still carrying Shannon—to the pasture and helped her down. She slipped and ended up grabbing onto his shoulders to steady herself. Grant was A-okay with that, and grinned down at her.

A beautiful blush stained her cheeks as she stepped back —and met the horse, who still hadn't moved.

"Go on, Crossfire." The horse plodded away, joining Gwyneth in the pasture, and Grant took Shannon to a grassy spot under one of the aspen trees that had the most leaves. Bullseye slurped from the stream and then laid down in the shade several feet away.

"Ah," Grant sighed as he sat and leaned against the tree trunk. "This is nice."

She cuddled into his side, and he took a breath of her floral and sweet scent and closed his eyes, tipping his hat forward as he rested his head on the bark. "It is."

"So is Gwyneth going to be a problem?"

"I told her what's what." Shannon's breath drifted across his forearm, and Grant played with her hair, thrilled at the connection he felt with her, the easiness of being with her, the peace pulling through him.

"So what do you do in the summer?" he asked.

"Principals still work," she said. "I'll be at the school all of June, obviously, because we do summer school. I take time off in July, and I'm back by the beginning of August."

"So you get July off. What do you do then?"

"My sister and I usually go on a cruise." She stiffened in his arms, and he heard the cooler note in her voice when she said, "Or we used to."

"Used to?"

"She's...upset with me right now."

Grant sensed a much bigger story behind those simple words, and he gave Shannon several seconds of silence to start the tale. She didn't.

As the ease between them evaporated, Grant grasped for it, wanting to bring it back. He didn't want Shannon to feel any amount of pain or heartache. "So you're not perfect," he said.

"What?" She pushed away from him enough to look into his face. If he just leaned down, just a little, he felt sure she'd stretch up to meet his mouth.

He swallowed and said, "For the first few weeks there, I couldn't find any flaws."

She blinked and there were no barriers between them. "That's why my sister is mad at me."

"Oh?"

"She thinks I'm jealous. See, she was engaged, and... then things fell apart, and she blamed me."

"You?"

Shannon sighed and resignation crossed her expression. "Her fiancé hit on me at my mom's house last Labor Day. I told Hannah, and she didn't believe me. Her fiancé left town and never came back, but somehow the end of the relationship is still my fault."

She leaned back into him, and Grant's heart beat, and beat, and beat. "I'm sorry," he said.

"So she thinks I'm a little devious, a lot jealous, and really arrogant."

Grant rubbed small circles on her upper arm. "I can't

even imagine you as any of those things. You are really strong. Intimidating."

Shannon bolted upright. "Intimidating?"

He realized he'd said the wrong thing. Totally wrong. But the word was out, and he couldn't suck it back in. "Just a little."

"In what way?" Her gaze sharpened.

"In that way," he said, gesturing toward her as he swallowed. "You're drop-dead gorgeous, for one. That's intimidating to a man like me. You're powerful, successful, educated, organized. It's a little unnerving." Why hadn't he stopped talking yet?

"*Was. Was* unnerving," he tried to correct himself. He pressed his lips together, determined not to speak again.

She narrowed her eyes at him. "A man like you? What kind of man are you?"

He shrugged, fully committed to remaining silent. He didn't think he could fit anymore foot inside anyway.

She glared at him. After a few seconds, everything in her relaxed. "You're right."

"I'm not right," he said robotically. "I'm rarely right. Just ask Landon."

"I work really hard to put all the pieces of myself in place."

"And I appreciate it."

She nudged him with her shoulder, and he chuckled. "I'd like you without those pieces in place," he said. "And I'm really glad you're scared of horses, and wearing the totally wrong shoes for a ranch, and that your sister is mad at you."

She giggled. "Stop it."

"No, really. It makes you more human." He kept his smile in place and dipped his head toward hers. "And I think you could probably trust a man who kissed you after the second date."

She jolted away from him like a bolt of electricity had passed through her.

Grant gazed at her, a tiny smile on his lips and a galloping heart in his chest. "What do you think?"

CHAPTER 7

W hat did Shannon think? At the moment, she could barely put a coherent thought together. She managed to say, "I think you should've kissed me last night."

"Should've?"

"I wanted you to."

"I wanted to as well." In one swift motion, he tightened his arm around her, drew her closer, and swiped his hat completely off his head. Only a moment later, he paused, his mouth only a millimeter from hers.

He touched his lips to hers for only a breath, barely long enough for her to feel anything. He growled and finally kissed her properly.

Shannon pressed into him, eagerly experiencing him in a whole new way. Maybe it had been a while since she'd kissed a man, but this kiss made her feel like the earth was spinning really fast. Either that, or super slow.

No matter what, she didn't think she'd ever been kissed so completely in all her life.

He broke their connection before she was ready, a chuckle lingering in the space between them. She wanted to kiss him again, so she did.

When she broke their contact this time, he leaned his forehead against hers. "I need to know a few more of your flaws."

"Yeah? Why's that?"

He slid his hand up her arm to the back of her neck. "Because it's incredibly unfair that you're so good at everything you do."

"You kinda liked that, didn't you?"

He kissed her again, and it was all the testimony she needed that he liked her. They stayed under the tree for a while longer, and then Grant said they had to get the horses back. Really, Shannon thought he was worried about his dog, who lay prostrate on the ground under the neighboring tree. His chest rose and fell in a fast pant, and as Shannon dusted off her jeans, she nodded to the white bulldog.

"Is he going to make it back?"

Grant looked at his dog. "Bullseye."

The dog didn't lift his head. He did slightly use his neck to gaze at Grant with the biggest puppy dog eyes Shannon had ever seen. She went over to the dog and stroked him. "You okay, bud?"

He licked her hand and she giggled. "You're a sweetheart, aren't you?"

"He's a good little dog." Grant bent down and rubbed the dog's back. "We gotta get back, Bullseye. I'm starving." He glanced at Shannon. "You busy tonight? Want to go to dinner?"

She liked his proximity, the way he gazed at her with softness in the edges of his eyes, the scent of the woods he carried in his skin. "Dinner sounds great. I could cook for us."

"You cook?"

"Sometimes." She laughed. "I don't know what I'm saying. Making a meal for me is grilling asparagus or making a fruit protein shake." She shook her head, unsure of where her brain had gone. She hadn't gone this dumb over a man in, well, ever. "Forget I said that. Let's order pizza or something though."

"You don't want to go out?"

"I have a great backyard," she said. "You could bring Bullseye. He can play with my two dogs."

"You have two dogs? Where were they earlier?"

"In the backyard." She stood and glanced around for her horse. She couldn't see either animal anywhere and blip of panic pinged through her.

"I like pizza, and Bullseye loves other dogs."

"I have a nosy neighbor," Shannon said, going for full disclosure.

"Another flaw." He slipped his hand into hers. "Now where have those horses got to?"

————

A COUPLE OF HOURS LATER, Shannon pulled into her garage, Grant's truck behind her. She couldn't remember a more perfect day. She'd puttered around the house in the morning, even going so far as to clear the budding weeds from her flowerbeds. She paid a twelve-year-old boy to come mow her lawn, and he started next week.

"Let's go," he said and Bullseye spilled out of the truck.

Shannon went into the house and continued past the dining room table she rarely used and into the kitchen. She found both her dogs waiting for her at the sliding glass door, which she opened to wagging tails and slobbering tongues.

"Hey, guys." She scrubbed them and gave Bear a little extra hug. "Hey. Did you have a good afternoon without me? Where's that tennis ball, huh?" She glanced into the backyard, but she didn't see it.

Bullseye joined the fray and the dogs circled and sniffed. Sniffed some more. Theo barked, and Shannon shushed him before saying, "Go on. Go run." She nudged Bear back outside, and the other two dogs went with him.

She turned to Grant, a bit self-conscious to have him here though he'd come last night. "So, pizza?"

"I like the combo kind."

She called in the order, glad Grant liked the same kind of pizza as her. One of her past boyfriends insisted on ham and pineapple, and Shannon couldn't stomach hot fruit. So they'd always order two pizzas for two people, and she'd hated that. She'd dated him for another three months before calling it quits.

But at this moment, she couldn't think of a single reason why she wouldn't want to be with Grant. She hung up with the only pizza joint in town and went into the backyard, Grant right behind her.

She picked up a ball and threw it to the dogs. Bear went

nuts for a ball, but Theo didn't seem to notice it. Bullseye frolicked around like he'd gone to doggy heaven.

"Can I ask you a question?" Grant stepped to her side.

"Sure." Bear bounded back to her. "Drop it," she said, and the dog dropped the ball at her feet. She picked it up, a pulse of anxiety soaring through her. She tossed the ball, sending Bear tearing after it.

"Will you sit with me at church tomorrow?"

Shannon laughed, the relief rushing through her too strong.

"What?" he asked.

"I thought you were going to ask something hard," she said. "Church is easy."

"Oh, well, I wasn't sure, you know, because you haven't seemed interested in sitting by me before."

Shannon ignored Bear, who circled her with the ball clenched in his jaws. "I didn't know you wanted me to."

"Where I come from, bringing a woman to church means you're serious."

Shannon's surprise lifted her eyebrows. "Really?"

"That's what my momma taught me. Otherwise, church is for worshipping God."

The only sound in the backyard was the labored breathing of dogs. Shannon stepped around Bear to get closer to Grant. "So if you sit by me, you won't be able to worship?"

"It'll be harder," he admitted, his hand landing on her waist and sending a tremor down her spine. "You distract me in the best way possible." His throaty whisper and the emotion in his words half-terrified and half-excited her.

She grinned up at him, wondering how they'd lived in

the same town for three years and had never met. All she could think about was kissing him again.

"So it's okay for us to sit together?"

"I don't see why not."

"Wasn't sure if the job had anything to do with it."

Shannon hadn't exactly forgotten about the job, but she hadn't thought about how that would look either. She'd submitted his hire paperwork just yesterday. But her supervisor didn't live in Brush Creek, and Shannon could date whoever she wanted.

What's the right thing to do here? she thought, hoping the Lord would answer quickly. She didn't feel much of anything, which for her, usually meant her own judgment was good enough.

"It's fine," she said, thinking of snuggling up to him in a church pew. She definitely wouldn't be able to focus much on the pastor's sermon with Grant so close, his hand in hers or his arm around her shoulders.

She couldn't remember the last time she'd felt this giddy about a relationship, and it felt nice. She felt for the first time since her falling out with Hannah that maybe she was worth something, that perhaps she would be able to find some measure of happiness.

She hadn't realized how deep Hannah's accusations and silence had cut her until confronted with her empty house every night. Grant found her intimidating, sure. But not completely unapproachable. And Shannon had never thought she was a jealous person—but she'd been second-guessing herself for months.

"Want me to come pick you up in the morning, or do you want to meet there?"

She rather liked the idea of him coming to get her, so she said, "Come get me," and tipped up onto her toes to kiss him, the three dogs watching.

At least until she heard the gasp and the squeak of the tool chest on the other side of the fence. Ruth had seen her, and a fair amount of panic pooled in her gut.

Doesn't matter, she told herself as Grant tucked her against his chest and chuckled at the dogs. Ruth would find out--along with the whole town--tomorrow when she strutted into the chapel with a new accessory on her arm.

Chapter 8

"What's goin' on?" Emmett stood on Grant's front porch, his arms folded, and his wife Molly in the truck idling in the lane.

"Nothing."

"You haven't come to church with us for three weeks."

"I'm going, just…by myself." Until today, that was true.

"What's this about?"

Emmett would watch him like one of those action comedies he loved so much. Grant couldn't very well lie about it. Didn't want to.

"I'm picking up Shannon Sharpe."

The other cowboy's eyes widened. "Oh yeah?"

"It's nothing," Grant said though a smile spread his lips just thinking about the last kiss he'd shared with Shannon.

"Yeah, I can see that by the way you're smiling like you just won the lottery."

Grant's smile faltered. Emmett couldn't know that Grant had bought dozens of lottery tickets, trying to get the money he needed to pay his debts. He hated that a simple conversation could so easily remind him of his past mistakes.

"It's not nothing," Emmett said while Grant reminded himself that he'd given up gambling when he'd come to Brush Creek. "With all the women you've dated, I've never known you to sit by them at church."

Grant shrugged. "That's because…well, a lot of reasons." Some of the women he'd dated had lived in neighboring towns, but it wasn't like he didn't have a working vehicle. Some of them hadn't been terribly religious. Some of them he just didn't want to parade around on his arm. "I'll see you there, okay?" He nudged Bullseye to back up into the house, and he drew the door closed in Emmett's grinning face.

Grant leaned against the door and took a deep breath. Landon would see him with Shannon. Ted. Walker. Everyone in the town.

"I want them to," he muttered to himself as he went back into his bathroom to finish getting ready. True, he hadn't known Shannon for long, but he enjoyed her company more than anyone else's.

As he drove down the canyon, Grant's stomach buzzed like someone had poured an entire beehive down his throat. Every breath felt sticky, and his hands slipped on the steering wheel. He couldn't seem to swallow properly. He mentally coached himself to calm down, but it wasn't until he sent a prayer heavenward that he finally managed to take a breath that felt properly oxygenated.

He pressed Shannon's doorbell, unsurprised to hear a custom chime sound behind the door. Her heels clicked against her floor and a moment later, she opened the door and leaned into it. "Hey." A smile oozed over her face, making Grant's heart pump extra hard and feel very vulnerable.

"Hey." He grinned goofily back at her for several long moments before putting himself back together. "You ready or should I come in?"

She glanced next door and Grant followed her gaze but found only a red minivan sitting in the driveway.

"I'm ready," she said, stepping out of the house and joining him on the front steps. She glanced up at him, and it could've been his imagination, but it seemed like her smile was a little wobbly.

Neither one of them could find anything to say on the short ride to the church, and Grant's nerves kicked into a new gear when he had to stop and wait for Claire to cross the parking lot in front of him before he found a space.

The other blonde looked up and her eyes moved in slow motion as they traveled from his face to Shannon's. Pure horror entered her expression at the same time Shannon sucked in a breath. Anxiety pulled through Grant. He wasn't exactly sure what Shannon's plan regarding Claire had been, but he didn't have anything to feel bad about.

After all, Claire had ended things with him, not the other way around. He still wasn't sure why, as she'd just cut off all contact one day, and when he'd asked why, all she'd said was that she didn't want to see him anymore.

Thus, the stalking had started at the elementary school. He wasn't sure what he'd thought he'd say or do if he ever came face-to-face with Claire. Thankfully, that hadn't happened.

"I take it she doesn't know about us." Grant pulled into an available space and killed the ignition.

"No one knows about us," Shannon said. "Well, my neighbor does. She caught us kissing in the back yard last night. And I'm assuming a friend or two of yours knows."

"One or two," Grant said.

Shannon played with the ends of her hair as she stared toward the church. "I guess it's time to show everyone else." She sighed as she got out of the truck, and Grant didn't like the sound of it.

"I can just sit by my friends," he said.

"Did I say I wanted you to sit by your friends?"

"I think this might be too soon for you," he said.

She glared even as she tucked her arm in his. "I'm not embarrassed to be with you." She paused her step and looked up at him. "Are you embarrassed to be with me?"

"Of course not."

"Then let's go." She lifted her eyebrows as if she expected him to bolt.

He stepped toward the chapel instead. He was sure not every eye landed on them as they entered and found an empty spot on the left side, but it sure felt like it. Most of them belonged to a cowboy or a woman, and Grant kept his shoulders straight and his face toward the pulpit as he waited for Shannon to settle onto the pew.

He joined her, threading his fingers through hers and taking a deep breath of her floral perfume. That scent calmed him, as did the organ music, and when Pastor Peters got up and started speaking, Grant forgot about everyone staring at him.

Pastor Peters had a way with words, and he said things

in a simple way so Grant could understand. Today he said, "One of the greatest blessings of forgiveness is that we don't have to own that sin anymore." He swept his gaze from left to right, front to back. "What the Lord forgives, He forgets. We should too."

Grant found himself nodding, muttering "Amen," and realizing that he hadn't actually done that for himself. He still thought of himself as the loser-cowboy who'd come coasting into town on gas fumes, hoping a stranger who was a rodeo friend of a rodeo friend would give him a job.

Landon had done that, and a whole lot more. Grant's gratitude had never run dry, and he believed he'd been forgiven for his past mistakes. What he hadn't done is forget about it. Move on. Look forward.

No, he'd been hiding. Hiding his secret from his friends on the ranch. Hiding it from every woman he dated. Hiding from himself.

He leaned over before he could even think about what he was about to say. "Hey, can we talk afterward?"

"I made lunch, remember?" She flicked her eyes from the pulpit to his. "I texted you about it. Barbeque pork sandwiches in my backyard."

"Right." He skated his lips across her brow. "I just don't want to forget to tell you something."

"What?" Her eyes hooked his this time.

"Later." He focused on Pastor Peters again, but he didn't hear anything else the preacher said. He'd never actually told anyone except Landon about his former financial fiasco. And he'd only told Landon because his bookie was in town, demanding his money.

The meeting ended, and Grant took a few extra seconds

before he stood. He figured Emmett would hightail it over to meet Shannon, and he wasn't disappointed.

"Grant, Molly wants to know what you guys are doing for lunch."

Molly stepped to his side, and her smile was genuine and warm. "I threw something in the crock pot this morning," she added.

"Oh, Shannon made lunch." Grant reseated his cowboy hat and looked at Shannon, who was a natural with people.

She wore an equally warm smile, and said, "Why don't you two join us at my place?"

Emmett looked at Grant, who shrugged and squeezed Shannon's hand. Molly looked at Emmett, and they must've learned how to read minds since they'd been married, because she said, "Yeah, we'd like that too."

Grant started toward the back of the chapel, almost desperate to leave now for a reason he couldn't name. He'd taken three steps when someone said, "Shannon, can I talk to you for a sec?"

He turned to find Claire standing several paces away, her arms clenched tight around her middle.

Shannon blinked at her, and then turned back to Grant. "Give me a few minutes, okay?" She slipped away from him, and while Grant had no idea what Claire needed to say to Shannon, his gut writhed like it had been magicked into a snake.

He paused at the door and turned back, but Emmett put his hand on Grant's shoulder and pushed. "Leave it. Trust me, you don't want to be in the middle of that."

Shannon stood with her back to Grant, so he couldn't see her face. She blocked Claire, and Grant couldn't determine anything just by looking. He once again reminded himself that he hadn't done anything wrong in the relationship with Claire. He'd genuinely liked her, had been truly upset when she'd ended things.

Still, he couldn't help worrying over what she was saying to Shannon that made her shoulders bunch like that.

CHAPTER 9

"I don't believe you," Shannon said. She couldn't. True, she didn't know Grant that well. Sending hundreds of texts and spending a few days together didn't make her an expert on the man. At the same time, she couldn't believe he'd gamble away his entire rodeo winnings, his whole life, before showing up broke and broken in Brush Creek. He had to be smarter than that.

More than anything else, Claire looked sad, and Shannon didn't know what to do with that. She didn't seem vindictive. Angry. Just...sad. "It's why I decided to end things with him," she said, reaching out and touching Shannon's forearm. Claire had started teaching the same year Shannon had been given her first administrative assignment at Brush Creek. Shannon herself had taught for six years, three of which she'd worked on her administrative endorsement and applied to be a principal.

Shannon stared at the other woman's perfectly manicured fingernails. Vaguely, she heard Claire say, "I want someone who can take care of me, not the other way around."

"I can take care of myself," Shannon said. "I have to go." She turned and marched up the aisle, her words practically ringing in the rafters. She could take care of herself. She'd been doing it for thirty-four years. Once she hit the lobby, she detoured into the ladies' room to make sure all the pieces she used to put herself together were still in place.

Her eyes looked a little more watery than usual, but her makeup was flawless. Her gold hoops sparkled in the light. Her blouse lay exactly right, with the pink parts of the necklace showing right along her collarbone.

Staring at herself, she realized how tired she was. Tired of being this perfect version of Shannon Sharpe. She wanted to roll out of bed on Saturday mornings and wear her pajamas all day while Theo and Bear chased a ball.

Would Grant care if she did that?

No, a voice whispered in her head. She could barely hear it above the sound of her ticking, ticking, ticking biological clock. She wanted a family, and she wanted to be there to raise them. If Grant really couldn't support her, would she have to work outside the home?

"I don't want that," she whispered to herself. But she couldn't just believe Claire either. She drew in a deep breath and determined to do what she'd do at school: Get both sides of the story.

Satisfied, she exited the bathroom and entered the sunshine. Grant waited for her against his truck, and when he saw her, he pushed to a standing position and approached with long strides. He wore his anxiety openly on his face, and Shannon adored that.

He cared about her.

He cares about me. The thought felt like helium to her soul, lifting her spirits toward the clouds.

"Everything okay?" He reached her and ran his warm hands up her arms.

"Sort of," she said, wondering how she brought up this rumor. Maybe he'd simply tell her. If he was as serious about her as she hoped he was, he'd want her to know everything about his life, right?

"What did Claire say?"

"She told me why she broke up with you."

"Wow." Grant looked over Shannon's head toward the church. "I don't even know that."

"What do you mean?"

"I mean she sent me a text one morning saying she didn't want to see me anymore. When I asked her why, she never responded. I don't know what I did." He stepped with her and they moved to the truck. He opened the door and she climbed in, holding one hand over the back of her skirt so she didn't flash him.

He got in beside her and put his hands on the wheel, but he didn't put the truck in gear. "So, what did she say?"

Shannon thought he carried a bit too much interest in his voice. He was over Claire, wasn't he?

Of course he is, she chastised herself. She'd already asked that question, and she believed Grant. She believed *in* Grant.

"I didn't really understand it," she said. "Can we talk about something else?"

"Sure." Always the easy-going cowboy, Grant turned up the radio, the sound of country twang almost too loud to think through. Shannon couldn't make what Claire had claimed about him line up with the man sitting beside her. Pastor Peters' words from the sermon only minutes ago slammed into her.

Of course she couldn't make the accusation of who he was years ago line up with who he was today. He'd changed.

"And people deserve to make mistakes," she muttered.

"What?"

"Nothing."

He reached for her hand, and she willingly gave it to him. It had only been three weeks since she'd strode over to him and told him to leave the school grounds. She didn't have to know everything about him right now. What she did know, she liked, and what she'd seen, she admired. She'd wait until he told her, and then she'd know how serious about her he was.

Once at her house, Shannon flew into guest gear. She got down her best dishes and asked Grant to set the table. When Emmett and Molly showed up, Grant recruited Emmett to table duty and Molly stepped into the kitchen. "Anything I can do to help?"

Shannon grinned at the taller woman. "Stir this barbeque sauce?" She handed her the wooden spoon.

"You made your own barbeque sauce?" Molly stared at her like Shannon had grown a set of horns on her forehead. "I didn't know people even did that."

Shannon giggled to cover up the fact that she didn't normally cook this elaborately. She'd just wanted her first homecooked meal for Grant to leave an impression. Seemed like it would accomplish that, at least.

"It was super easy. Dump this in, measure in some spice. Done."

Molly still seemed dubious as she stirred, and Shannon opened her second crock pot to shred the pork.

"Coleslaw is in the fridge," she told Grant, who retrieved it and put it on the table.

"And buns right here." She nodded to a package on the counter. "Knives there. They need to be sliced."

Emmett took over that job while Shannon transferred the shredded pork to a large bowl. "Barbeque sauce here."

Molly let her take over the job of mixing the meat and the sauce, and then Shannon said, "Dinner's ready." She wasn't sure she'd be able to eat more than a few bites as quaky as her stomach seemed to be. She forced a smile to her face and looked around at her company.

A pang of homesickness hit her. It had been so long since she'd cooked for someone besides herself. She hadn't visited her mom in Atlanta since the Labor Day incident, and emotion choked in her throat.

"Thanks for coming," she said, and Grant's eyes flew to hers. He could hear her distress, and she waved it away with a small laugh. "Grant, would you say grace?"

Everyone sat down at the table, and Grant prayed, and Shannon found herself wishing this was her reality every Sunday. Every weekday. For always and forever.

Grant's hand found hers under the table and he squeezed, a quick question of "You okay?"

She smiled at him and plucked a bun from the basket in front of her. "I hope you guys like Saint Louis style barbeque."

"I don't even know what that means," Emmett said. "But it smells great."

"She made the barbeque sauce," Molly said, scooping some coleslaw onto her plate. "From scratch."

"You can do that?" Grant asked, and Shannon tipped her head back and laughed.

———

"I thought they'd never leave." Grant turned from the closed front door, where Emmett and Molly had just left.

"I like them." Shannon picked up two coffee cups. She couldn't remember a better Sunday afternoon.

"Remember I wanted to talk to you?"

She almost dropped the mugs but managed to set them in the sink before facing him again. "Oh, right."

He invaded her personal space, and she didn't mind. Her hands went automatically to his chest, and she seemed to fit right next to him.

"Did you like the sermon today?" he asked.

"I always like hearing about forgiveness." She tried on a quick smile. "I'm hoping Hannah will forgive me one day."

The intensity in his eyes softened the tiniest bit. "I'm one of those people Pastor Peters was talking about."

"What do you mean?"

"I mean I've done some things in my life I'm not proud of, and I've worked through them." He cleared his throat. "Been forgiven. But I haven't forgotten about them yet. One of them is still haunting me. I can't really forget about it until—" He cleared his throat and swiped his cowboy hat off his head. "I mean, I know I'm good with God, but with Landon...."

Shannon had no idea what he was talking about. She gave him the time he needed to organize and articulate what he needed to. This tactic usually worked with kids.

He searched her eyes, but she didn't know what to give him. "I'm not making much sense, am I?"

"I'm afraid not," she whispered.

He inhaled deeply, his chest puffing out beneath her hand. "After I left the rodeo, I sort of wandered around lost for a while. I—I liked to gamble, especially on horses. I lost all my winnings, and more. I was in a real bind, running from those I owed money to, until I landed here in Brush Creek."

Shannon could only blink, and only because it was an involuntary bodily function. Claire had been telling the truth.

"Landon and I have a mutual friend in the rodeo, and he told me to come to the horse ranch and see if Landon would give me a job." Pure agony shone in Grant's eyes, and Shannon wanted to kiss it away, make it so he didn't have to feel this kind of pain anymore.

"He gave me more than that. He gave me the money I needed to get square with everyone, and now I just pay him back."

"How much do you still owe him?" Shannon asked.

"I'll be done payin' at the end of this year." He sagged against the countertop as if he needed it to support him. "Then I think I'll be ready to forget and move on."

She liked the sound of that, but the end of the year suddenly seemed so far away. She stretched up and kissed him, but he didn't melt into her the way he usually did. "Thanks for telling me."

He exhaled, the more carefree and gentle Grant she'd come to like replacing that serious, stern-faced version of him. "I'm sorry."

"You don't have anything to apologize for. We all make mistakes."

He eased away from her and gathered the last two mugs from the living room. "Are you always this understanding?"

"Usually," she said. "It comes with the territory of dealing with small humans all day long."

"Do you like being a principal?"

"Most days." She began to load the dishes from lunch into the dishwasher. "Just not in May or September. Or December. Or—"

Grant burst out laughing. "You just named half the months in the school year."

She straightened and met his eye. "I've been in Brush Creek for a while," she said.

"And?"

"And most principals get moved to different schools throughout their careers. This is just an assignment. A temporary one."

A frown marred his whole face. "Are you saying you could be leaving?"

"Not *could be*," she said. "I was actually expecting a transfer this year. I'd be shocked if one didn't come for next year."

"Where will you go?"

"I don't get to choose."

"What are the options?"

"The district is pretty big. Could be up to an hour away."

"Oh, an hour." His joviality came back. "I can handle an hour."

Maybe he could, but Shannon was beginning to wonder if she could survive without him at her side all the time.

CHAPTER 10

Grant didn't know revealing secrets could be so liberating. He imagined it felt a lot like forgetting about the wrongs he'd done in the past. Once he'd paid back Landon every dime—plus interest— he'd know what that felt like.

The high pushed him through the next few weeks where he only saw Shannon on weekends, where they spent a large portion of their time planning the summer school afternoon activities—and kissing. There was always kissing on the weekends.

Bullseye took to lying around the cabin in a state of depression for days after a good playdate with her dogs, and Grant understood the animal's feelings. He puttered around his cabin on the weeknight evenings, wondering what she was making for dinner and if she missed him as much as he pined for her.

Thankfully, she seemed to hold an advanced degree in texting, and he'd figured out a pattern for her, since she never messaged at school. If there was someone who worked more than cowboys did, it was a principal, as Shannon rarely texted before six pm.

Tonight's read *School's out on Friday! Let's celebrate.*

Grant wanted to know how Shannon celebrated such a thing, so he asked *What do you want to do?*

Surprise me.

Grant groaned, the sound loud in his silent cabin. He had no idea how to surprise a woman like Shannon, who'd taken cruises with her sister for years. Who tamed hundreds of children and ran a constantly moving ship of teachers, aides, and custodians. Who knew how to make lasagna with eggplant.

He almost texted back to say he didn't do surprises, but erased the message. He didn't want her to think he was unromantic, or didn't know her, or wasn't excited that school was out this Friday.

Feeling frantic, he said, "C'mon, Bullseye," and stepped outside. Summer had almost arrived in Brush Creek, and the trees boasted full foliage, the grass was emerald green from the April rains, and everything smelled fresh and clean. Well, as clean as a horse ranch could smell.

He trekked across the gravel lane to the homestead, hoping he could catch both Landon and Megan at the same time. He knocked and entered at the same time. "Hello?"

Megan glanced up from where she sat at the kitchen counter. "Come on in, Grant. Landon's in the backyard with the kids."

She looked tired, and Grant almost thanked her and left her alone—which she clearly wanted. But something whispered to stop and talk to her.

"Hey," he said. "I actually came to talk to you."

She abandoned her book and turned toward him. "What's going on?"

"So I'm dating Shannon Sharpe, right?"

"Right." Megan grinned at him. "Is it going well?"

"Well enough," he said. "School gets out on Friday, and she wants me to surprise her." He held out his phone so she could see the texts.

Megan finished reading and whistled. "What are you going to do?"

"That's why I'm here. What do you think?"

"I barely know Shannon Sharpe. I mean, the girls go to school there, but we've had very little interaction with her."

"But you're a woman. What would you like?"

"A romantic weekend in Salt Lake City without the kids," she answered immediately. "Maybe go to the symphony, dinner I don't have to cook, shopping, sleeping in." She sighed and her eyes took on a faraway quality.

Grant chuckled nervously, thinking of Shannon in a swimming suit on a cruise ship. Even if he could afford such a thing, they weren't married and couldn't possibly take a weekend trip together. Could they?

"I realize that won't work for you," she said. "Let's see." She turned thoughtful and after several prolonged moments, she said, "I'll ask the other ranch wives." She reached for her phone before Grant could stop her.

"No, I—"

Her thumbs flew and she put the phone down. "Done."

Grant's hopes deflated a little. "I don't want everyone to know."

"Know what? That you're dating Shannon? Everyone already knows that, silly."

He folded his arms and leaned his weight on his back foot. "That I don't know how to surprise her."

Megan laughed. "Grant, don't worry about it. I gave up on surprises from Landon a while ago, though he does still manage to do something that makes me fall in love with him all over again." She wore a small smile as she looked toward the sliding glass door. "We ranch wives have learned to tell our men what we want."

That sounded great to Grant. "When will Shannon do that?" he asked.

Megan grinned wickedly. "Probably in about the third year of your marriage."

Pure panic bolted through Grant. "Oh, we're not—I mean—marriage?" His voice came out as weak and rusty as an old hinge.

"Oh, we're not there yet." Megan covered her mouth in mock surprise. "At least *you* aren't." Her phone buzzed, stealing her attention away, but Grant could barely focus past the M-word. Did Shannon think about *marrying* him? He wasn't even sure how that was possible. And then what? She'd come live up here in his cowboy cabin and become a ranch wife? Did she even want such a thing?

He didn't know, which meant no, he wasn't anywhere near ready to talk marriage. He just needed a good surprise to help her celebrate the end of the school year.

"April says Shannon comes to her step class every week, and she can give you a certificate for a free month." Megan scanned the phone. "Tess said she'll make a cake that's all summery. Her exact words are 'every woman loves chocolate.'" Megan glanced up, but Grant was still reeling from the fact that Shannon went to a step class every week. There was so much he didn't know about her. Who was he kidding? How had he deluded himself to think he knew her at all?

"I have to go," he said. "Thanks, Megan."

"Wait! I think you should get her a massage gift certificate. She works hard, I bet. And Molly says don't make her cook for herself for a while. Renee suggested a cleaning service. And Erin—"

"I'll figure something out," Grant said, somewhat surprised that all the suggestions coming from the ranch wives were about making their lives more pampered. He crossed the lane, thinking he'd never once wished for a massage or someone to come clean his cabin. Now cake he could get behind, but he wasn't sure he wanted Tess to make it. She already did so much for everyone around her, and Grant didn't want to add more to her schedule with only a couple of days notice.

On Friday evening after work, he found a beautifully decorated cake sitting on his kitchen counter. It was decorated with a beach scene, with a bright yellow sun that screamed summer vacation. Next to it sat an envelope that held a massage gift certificate and the coupon for a free month of step classes with April.

Gratitude filled his whole soul at the loving kindness of his friends. He'd planned a romantic dinner but hadn't done much past that. Number one, he wasn't convinced someone like Shannon really wanted a stranger in her house or rubbing her down. She liked being in control, and he'd been forced to add "neat freak" to her list of flaws, because the fact was the woman had very few things she wasn't good at.

A note sat next to the items the ranch wives had brought over. *Take a chance* it read, sending Grant's heart into a frenzy.

He didn't take chances. He didn't make bets. He didn't do risky things. Not anymore. He didn't want to crave the rush of excitement when he won, or the disappointing devastation when he lost. It was better if he lived where there weren't wins or losses, nothing to gamble with, nothing to chance.

And yet somehow, he'd put his heart on the chopping block. Had he already lost it to Shannon Sharpe?

Something told him that yes, he definitely had gambled with his heart and had already lost it to a beautiful blonde.

CHAPTER 11

Grant was late—something that had never happened. Shannon had survived the last week of school by sheer willpower, and she'd clung to the thought of Grant whisking her away on a fun-filled surprise to get her through this last day.

And now he wasn't here. Hadn't called or texted.

Have fun on your date! Ruth messaged, but Shannon didn't have the heart to respond. So maybe she'd spent the past couple of evenings in her neighbor's backyard, detailing most details of her relationship with Grant. She'd had to do something once Ruth caught them kissing. And honestly, Shannon liked talking things through with another woman. Hannah had always been that person, and Shannon missed her more acutely than ever.

She went to the front window and checked outside. No truck. No Grant. She let the blinds drop and she sat in the armchair closest to the door so she'd know the instant his rumbly truck arrived.

Forty minutes later, Shannon jolted awake, having dozed off at some point. Something had woken her, and she glanced around as she tried to remember where she was and what she'd been doing.

Living room. Grant.

She lunged toward the blinds but had barely parted them before a knock sounded on the door. In the past, Grant had just walked right in, but he didn't this time. If it was even him.

Shannon hoped with everything she had that it was him. She hurried around the couch and opened the door, relief coating her at the sight of the handsome cowboy on her front porch.

"Hey," she said. "You're later than I expected."

"Yeah." He stuck his free hand in his pocket. In his other he carried a gorgeously decorated cake. He made no move to enter the house.

Shannon's mouth watered, both from the man and the dessert. She glanced up into his face, but he wouldn't look at her. She noticed the complete agony on his face, and all her hopes for the evening took a dive.

"Is everything okay?"

He shook his head and brushed past her. "I'll just put this stuff in the kitchen." He moved through her living room and set the cake on the counter. Next to it, he placed a few envelopes he extracted from his back pocket. "The ranch wives put this all together."

Shannon closed the door and followed him, her heart rocketing around in her chest. She slipped her fingers into his, but he pulled away quickly.

"I have to go."

"Go?" She moved in front of him so he couldn't rush out. "Why? I thought we were going to celebrate the last day of school tonight."

He chin-nodded toward the stash on the counter. "There's the celebration." He still wouldn't look at her, and Shannon felt very much like she was trying to hold onto smoke.

"What's wrong?" she asked.

He exhaled, letting the air out in a slow hiss between his teeth. "I don't think this is gonna work out between us."

Shannon fell back a step, sure she hadn't heard him right. Things had been going great. She liked him; he told her things about his life; she'd shared some of hers with him. Did she know everything about him? No. Did she want to? Very much so.

"Why not?"

He shrugged one shoulder and shoved both hands in his pockets. He reminded her so much of the way students shut down, and she suspected she'd get nothing out of him while he was in this state.

"What about summer school?" she asked.

"I can't do it," he said. "Landon needs me on the ranch."

Shannon had talked to Grant extensively about the summer program. She could do it herself, at least for the first week, if she had to. But it wasn't that loss that stung so harshly.

"So that's it." She wasn't asking. And she wasn't going to beg him to stay though everything inside her felt frantic. *What's going on?* she prayed. *What do I say here?*

"I guess so." He made to step around her, but she blocked him again.

"Are you going to tell me what I did wrong?"

He finally looked at her, his dark eyes glimmering like sunlight on murky water. "You did nothing wrong."

She put her hand on his chest. "Then what's going on? I like you. I thought you liked me. Things were going great."

Grant reached up and tucked her hair behind her ear, a gentle gesture that made her heart thrum and her tension to melt away. At least until he said, "I'm not ready for someone like you. I'm sorry, Shannon. You deserve someone better."

This time, when he tried to walk away, she let him.

———

SHANNON MANAGED to stumble next door and mutter a couple of words about what had happened.

"Did you say cake?" Ruth asked, holding onto Shannon's elbow like she was drunk and couldn't be trusted to stand.

"Big chocolate cake. I know it's chocolate because I slammed a knife right into the center of it." Everything in Shannon's life came into sharp focus then. She'd opened the envelopes and found all the things she did to pamper herself—massage certificate, free step classes, the works. Grant had said the ranch wives had put it together, and Shannon had gotten angry then.

Angry at herself. Angry at herself for putting so much pressure on Grant to come up with the perfect surprise for her. She'd never told him about the step classes, though they weren't a secret. But he'd obviously gone to outside sources looking for help with the surprise.

"Why didn't I just tell him I wanted him to take me to dinner and hold me on the couch?" She looked at Ruth, just now realizing she wasn't in her own house. "Why do I make every relationship so complicated?"

"Let's get you home and we'll talk." Ruth guided her to the door and into her own house. She set about cleaning up the scattered coupons and envelopes, as well as removing the vertical knife from the center of the cake. She cut two large slices and put them on paper plates before handing one to Shannon. "All right, tell me about it."

Shannon didn't know what else to say. She stabbed a large forkful of cake and shoved it in her mouth. Whoever had made this was a master with sugar and cocoa and milk. Whoever had made this wasn't Grant.

That made her angry too, and she set the slab of cake aside. She'd been out to the ranch several times over the past weeks, but she'd only met the owners, Megan and Landon. She wasn't even sure what a ranch wife was, but somehow she really wanted to be one.

She hadn't told Grant that either. In her experience, gushing about how much she wanted children usually drove men away. Of course, she'd done that without mentioning any of her dreams, or how loud her biological clock was ticking.

"I just want to know why," she finally said. Ruth nodded like she'd been privy to all the inner workings of Shannon's brain. "I didn't do anything wrong this time. We met five weeks ago. I saw him on the weekends. I never said anything about getting married, having kids, quitting my job. Nothing."

"You want to quit your job?"

Shannon shook her head, frustrated. "No. I mean, yes. I'd quit to have a family." She sighed, the end of the sound quaking. "I really want a family." She'd known that—had for a while. But she'd never said it out loud. It sounded different coming out of her mouth than it did circling in her head.

Ruth got up and took Shannon's cake back into the kitchen. "Shannon, do you really want a family *with him*?"

Numbness spread through her, and she held back the tears. "I don't know." She really wanted to talk to Hannah or her mom. Her mom went to bed early, but Hannah would still be awake. Shannon didn't know if she could handle the silence from her sister if she called, so she didn't make a move toward her phone.

Ruth returned and crouched in front of Shannon. "Are you in love with him?"

She shook her head, a single tear splashing down the side of her face. "It's been five weeks." She swiped at the tears, embarrassed at how easily she'd fallen apart. She hadn't even cried when Hannah had said all those terrible things and then stopped talking to her.

"So what? I fell in love with Richard in a weekend."

Shannon inhaled, trying to figure out how she felt and to order her thoughts. "But that's not me. I've never done that. I don't think I've ever even been in love." She met Ruth's eyes, and they were kind and clear. "What does being in love feel like?"

Ruth smiled the way Shannon imagined her mother

would. She reached out and wiped Shannon's tears too. "About like this, honey."

———

BY MONDAY, Shannon had fixed exactly one problem in her life: the summer school afternoon program. She'd gotten someone else to step in last-minute, and she'd met with the woman for two hours on Sunday evening.

In fact, she'd worked all of Sunday, the idea of going to church where she might see Grant too painful. She couldn't help wondering if he'd stayed away too.

She sat in her office, the first day well underway, finally with a moment to think. But she didn't like thinking. All her brain did was remind her of how utterly alone she was and that she'd never be a mother. She hadn't even realized how far she'd fallen with Grant. Didn't know she'd started to imagine living with him on the ranch and raising their children to romp through the fields and ride horses out to the stream and throw a ball with Bear, Theo, and Bullseye.

Feeling strong and somewhat insane, she picked up her phone. She hadn't shut Hannah out. Her sister had done that. Shannon had texted and called more times than she could count in the past ten months. She didn't want to give up on her sister. She wanted that door to be open any time Hannah wanted to walk through it.

She sent her sister a text: *Thinking about you. I need some advice. Maybe you could call me tonight?*

Without waiting for a reply, she fired off a message to Grant too. *Let's work through this. We've only been dating for five weeks. You can have as much time as you need.*

Hannah didn't respond.

But by lunchtime, Grant had. *This is about more than that.*

What's it about then? she asked.

And that was when Grant turned on the radio silence.

CHAPTER 12

Grant set Gwyneth in the pasture, shouldered his pack, and faced the cabin on the edge of the ranch property. He'd passed the stream an hour ago, and while he'd told Landon he'd check things out here—fence lines and the sprinkling system—he didn't feel like doing it today.

He somehow knew exactly what time it was, and that he should be at the elementary school right now, starting the summer extracurricular programs. He pushed the thoughts away and hiked up the path to the cabin.

He hadn't told anyone what he'd done on Friday night. He'd texted all the ranch wives a proper thank you from the safety of the parking lot at Oxbow Park, and he'd waited until late before driving back to the ranch. No one had questioned him over the weekend, and while Landon had given him a questioning cock of his right eyebrow, he hadn't said anything when Grant had volunteered to do the ranch work while everyone else went to church so the chores would be done that afternoon when they returned.

Grant had done that before, when he'd first come to Brush Creek. He'd been so worried about making sure Landon knew he was willing to work hard, to do whatever it took to pay back the favors Landon had blessed him with. He still was.

Only seven months left.

He'd spent the last forty-eight hours obsessing over his decision with Shannon. Maybe he'd been wrong. In the next moment, his resolve hardened and he was sure he'd absolutely made the right decision.

She *did* deserve someone better than him. He didn't own a house, or any property, or anything of worth. He'd once thought that someone like Shannon should be with a high-powered man, and that opinion hadn't changed despite knowing her better now.

They hadn't talked about marriage or a family yet, something Grant hadn't even thought of approaching. Of course, he hadn't realized how deep he'd gotten with Shannon, and he hadn't quite dared to admit to himself just how far down the hole went or how paralyzing his fear was.

He owned the break-up in other ways, and that had to be enough for now. He entered the cabin and a wall of stuffy air met him. He busied himself opening the windows and making sure he had somewhere to sleep when it got dark.

It was the first week of June, but once the sun went down, it would get chilly, so Grant made sure he had wood stacked next to the fireplace and he checked the generators to make sure he'd be able to keep his food cold and then get it hot when he wanted to. Satisfied he was ready to survive for the night, he finally went outside and navigated through the tall grass bolstered by the spring rains to the hammock.

He sighed as he sank into it, a moment of peace touching his soul. Only a moment, though, because as soon as he allowed himself to relax physically, his mind dug up everything about Shannon he was trying not to think about.

———

GRANT MADE it through exactly one week before Tess showed up on his front step. And she wasn't alone. Oh, no. Megan stood shoulder to shoulder with her, and April was crossing the lawn toward him.

He groaned and stepped back into the cabin, sweeping the women inside. Once the door closed behind April, he asked, "To what do I owe this honor, ladies?"

"Did you really break up with Shannon Sharpe?" Tess asked.

Megan put her hand on Tess's arm. "We were going to go in nice."

Tess took a breath and faced Grant again. He held up his hand before she could speak. "Yes, we broke up."

"*You* broke up with her."

"Tess," April said. "Why didn't you bake something and bring it over?"

"He doesn't deserve any treats." Her expression stormed with anger, and Grant wilted under the fierceness of it. He didn't want to explain himself. He couldn't. He didn't understand why Landon's innocent note had affected him so strongly, only that it had. He wasn't sure why he didn't believe in himself right now, only that he didn't.

"Did you even take her my cake?" Tess demanded.

"I am never inviting you to an intervention again," Megan said. She put her hand on Grant's elbow and guided him to the couch. Once they'd sat, she peered at him. He saw kindness in her eyes. Worry. Compassion. Curiosity.

"Was it something I said?" she asked.

"What? Megan, no." He shook his head. "No."

"Tess's cake was disgusting. That was it, right?"

Tess squeaked but didn't say anything else.

"Everything you guys did was great. I took everything down to her." Grant hung his hands between his knees, trying to figure out where he'd gone wrong. Where he'd gotten on a different road than Shannon.

"You don't like Shannon?"

"I like her a lot," he admitted.

"Why did you break up with her?"

"I don't know."

"You don't know?"

Grant looked at Megan, all his barriers down. He couldn't vocalize anything, and her sympathy should be used on someone else.

"Are you in love with her?"

Take a chance.

"I don't know."

April sat on the other side of him. "Then you could be."

Grant didn't even know which way was up anymore. He rubbed his face, his fingers scratching down his sideburns. "I have...things I'm still working on." He exchanged a glance with Megan.

"Those things don't matter," she said.

"Of course they do."

"Shannon won't care."

"*I* care."

Tess sat on the coffee table in front of Grant. "Are you just afraid?"

Grant met her eye, the first person besides Megan and Landon who had welcomed him to the ranch. She'd fed him more than he'd fed himself in the first six months he'd lived in Brush Creek. But even she didn't know about the gambling and the debts.

"Yes," he said simply. "And I don't take chances."

Megan flinched but recovered quickly. She stood and the other women did too. "You've got to let go of the past." She gave him a fast smile filled with half pain and half hope. "You're not the same man who showed up on my doorstep three years ago."

She left, taking the others with her. Grant stayed on the couch, her words on a constant loop in his ears. Even when Tess returned an hour later with freshly baked chocolate chip cookies. Even when his phone chimed and he saw Shannon's name.

He wanted to believe Megan, but he couldn't quite get there.

The following week, Grant didn't stay home from church. He didn't see Shannon there either, but he shouldn't have been too surprised. After all, they'd lived in the same town for three years, attended the same church, and he'd never seen her before either.

It hurt to sit in the pews without her at his side. Even the soothing voice of Pastor Peters couldn't erase the ache in his soul. He kept a prayer in his heart while he worked with the cattle, and he stayed on his knees longer than ever before crawling into bed.

No solutions to his Shannon problem had presented themselves.

It wasn't until the following week when the preacher said, "My brothers and sisters, we must first examine ourselves before we can examine others."

Grant wasn't entirely sure what that meant, and he'd been so deep in introspection that he could barely appreciate the summer sky above him. But those words shook something loose in his mind, and he realized that while he'd been examining himself all this time, he'd been inspecting the wrong version of himself.

Megan was absolutely right. He wasn't the Grant Ford who'd rolled into town a few years ago. Shannon hadn't seemed to care too much about his debts, and he hadn't even given her a chance—there was that nasty word again— to say if she'd live with him on the ranch or not. He didn't know if she wanted children—he didn't know if he did.

Maybe it's time I did take a chance, he thought. He glanced up to the chandelier hanging from the ceiling in the chapel, and the thought felt right. Good. For the first time in weeks, Grant finally found peace.

Soon enough, though, his anxiety returned, and he stood and slipped down a couple of rows to where Megan sat with her family. "Hey," he whispered.

"Grant." She handed her toddler to Landon and faced Grant. "What's going on?"

"How do I get Shannon back?"

Megan sucked in a breath and raised her eyebrows. "That's a tall order. You were supposed to plan a big surprise to celebrate the end of school and instead you broke up with her."

It sounded terrible said so plainly. Grant swallowed, and said, "How do I fix it?"

"I have no idea, but it'll have to be something big."

Something big. Grant nodded, checked the front of the chapel, and hurried out of the church. If he had to plan something big, he needed to get started right away.

CHAPTER 13

Summer school ended, and Shannon needed another celebration simply because she made it through the month without breaking down, hurting a child emotionally, or firing anyone—including herself.

She had one more meeting before her vacation began. Two bags sat by the exit leading to the garage, and while she wasn't going on her annual sister cruise, she was leaving town for three full weeks. Her first trip was taking her to Atlanta to visit her mother, and then she was planning to load up her car and go wherever she wanted to go. There was a lot of the United States she hadn't seen yet, and she had nothing but time.

She certainly didn't want to spend any time hanging around her house, alone except for two dogs. "C'mon guys," she called into the backyard. Bear came immediately, always the more obedient of the two. "Let's go. You're spending the summer with Carrie Ann."

One of her teachers, Carrie Ann had four cats and three dogs of her own, and she'd told Shannon several times that she wanted to quit teaching and open an animal daycare out of her house. Shannon thought that was all kinds of crazy, but she was glad Carrie Ann had agreed to take Bear and Theo for the next three weeks.

She had a twenty-five pound bag of dog food in her trunk, along with their leashes, toys, food and water bowls, and anything else she could think of that they needed. She drove toward the canyon, her eyes automatically following the road as far as she could before it curved.

She pulled her attention back to the neighborhood that sat at the base of the mountain and pulled into Carrie Ann's driveway. The third grade teacher came through the gate wearing a pair of shorts and a pink tank top along with a smile.

"Let's go guys." The dogs happily exited the car and trotted over to Carrie Ann, who was an obvious natural with animals. She put them in the backyard and helped Shannon unload their supplies. "I didn't bring a kennel," Shannon said. "They can sleep outside."

"They'll be fine. They can sleep in the laundry room with my dogs, or on the couch. Whatever."

Shannon smiled, already missing her dogs though she also craved the freedom to do whatever she wanted for the next twenty-two days. "Thank you so much, Carrie Ann."

"Sure, anytime."

Shannon gave her an envelope with the payment, and Carrie Ann tucked it into a drawer before going into the backyard. Shannon followed, momentarily stunned into silence by the display of doggie amazingness before her.

Carrie Ann had built a ball pit into a corner of her yard. A ball pit. Shannon stared at it as Bear frolicked through it, tossing balls in all directions with a look of pure joy on his face. Where most people had a tire swing or a hammock hanging from their tree limbs, Carrie Ann had an assortment of ropes tied into big knots. A giant mastiff currently bit a blue rope, growled, tossed his head, and sent the rope swinging. He went after it again as Shannon started laughing.

"Carrie Ann," she said once she'd stopped. "You need to turn in your resignation immediately. This is what you should be doing."

Carrie Ann looked at her with wide, brown eyes. "You really think so?"

Shannon gestured to the topsy turvy structure on the patio, covered in carpet, where three cats currently perched. "I've never seen anything like this. Pets are in heaven here. My dogs won't want to leave."

Theo came over to her and nosed her palm, making her feel like maybe he'd still come home with her at the end of her trip. Bear though....

"I'm not sure I could pay my bills." Carrie Ann tucked her hands in her back pockets and surveyed the yard. A deep, round pool took up the back corner of the yard, a clear place for dogs to cool off in the summer heat.

"Maybe it's time to have a little faith." Shannon flashed a tight smile, because she needed to take her own advice and didn't want to admit it—to herself or anyone else. She thanked Carrie Ann again and headed home.

A few days later, she'd crossed the country in relative safety. She entered the city proper of Atlanta, and her heart absolutely would not stay inside its proper place. Hannah lived in the city too, and while her mom had told Shannon that she'd begged Hannah to move past this rift between them, she didn't hold much hope.

Shannon had been clinging to a tiny thread of hope until her mom had told her that. Now she wasn't sure if she'd ever talk to her sister again. The thought had caused Shannon to take a personal day in the middle of summer school, something she'd never done before. Her personal life didn't affect her work. Never had—until now.

And it wasn't only Hannah making Shannon moody and depressed. She set aside her thoughts of Grant and continued through the city to her mother's house. She hadn't seen her mom in too long, and her tongue felt three sizes too large as she pulled into the driveway.

She honked and barely had the car in park before leaping from it. Her mom burst from the house, a giant grin on her face, and flew down the front steps to sweep Shannon into a tight hug. She laughed and said, "Oh, my sweet. It's so good to see you."

Shannon held onto her mom for dear life, like she was a life preserver and the ship was sinking fast. "Mom." Her voice came out halfway between a whisper and a whimper. While Shannon hadn't grown up in Atlanta, in this house, as she went inside with her mom and smelled roasting meat with a hint of leftover oatmeal cookie, she felt at home.

She settled at the counter while her mom put a pot on the stove and filled it with water. "So how was the school year?"

"You know," Shannon said, sighing. "School." She'd never felt like she didn't want to go back to school, but at the moment, the last place she wanted to be was her office. And she didn't want to talk about her job either.

Her mom seemed to pick up on that vibe, because she asked, "Seeing anyone?" next.

Shannon groaned. She didn't want to talk about that either. "No." Maybe if she kept her answers to one word, her mom would move on to her own job, and her own dating adventures. She'd recently delved into the world of online dating, and Shannon was starting to think maybe she'd give it a whirl. She had a million school photos, after all.

"What about you?" Shannon asked, hoping to put the spotlight somewhere else. "Who's interesting on the Internet these days?"

Her mom rolled her eyes and slid a second potato peeler across the counter. "Come help, and I'll tell you all about the *interesting* men you can find online."

Shannon smiled, and for the first time since Grant had shown up with stiff shoulders and horrible words, she didn't feel so twisted inside out.

By the end of the evening, though, Shannon wasn't sure she could wear her happy-brave-carefree mask for much longer. She yawned and got up from the couch where she'd been chatting with her mom for the past couple of hours. "I'm going to head to bed." She leaned over and hugged her mom. "Thanks for having me, Mom."

She'd only taken two steps when her mom said, "When are you going to tell me about the cowboy you were dating?"

Shannon froze and turned back to the couch. "What?"

"You mentioned him a couple of times." Her mom looked up, her gaze all-knowing. "And now you're not seeing anyone? I don't believe it. You can't hide things from your mother."

Shannon collapsed back to the couch and clasped her hands together. "Things were going great. Then he broke up with me on the last day of school." That was hands down one of the best and worst days of her life, all rolled into one.

"What happened?"

Shannon shrugged, her shoulders seemingly too heavy to lift more than an inch or two. "I don't know. He said I deserved someone better." She slumped back into the couch. "I'm never going to get married and have a family."

The emotion she'd been suppressing for weeks lingered so close to the surface, and the tiniest slip in the dam she used to keep everything bottled up let a steady stream of longing and loss rushing out.

"Don't say that," her mom said. "You'll meet someone new."

"I don't want to meet someone new." Shannon had never said that about someone she'd broken up with. She didn't even know it about Grant until she spoke.

"Is that so?" Her mom twisted toward her now, putting her knitting down completely. "Tell me about this guy."

And because Shannon wanted to talk about Grant, she started speaking.

———

THE WEEK with her mom passed with a lot of laughter, a load of comfort, and a league of love. Shannon felt like she could make it through another school year after spending time with her mom and she vowed not to let so much time pass before she visited again.

On the eve of her departure, they had reservations at one of her mom's favorite restaurants, and her mom insisted they wear their fanciest clothes. For Shannon, who was traveling, that meant a teal and gray sundress with gold sandals. They'd gotten pedicures, and her mom had done her makeup, the way she used to when Shannon was a teenager.

She felt glamorous and put together, the way she did when she went to school. Tonight, it didn't feel like a wet blanket, pressing on her lungs, the way it had in Brush Creek. They sat down, and she said, "I think I might be ready to leave Brush Creek."

"Oh yeah?" Her mom straightened her skirt and glanced up as the waiter arrived with water glasses. Three water glasses. Shannon eyed the third one, unsure of who was joining them. Her mom hadn't said anything.

"I thought you loved Brush Creek."

"I do," Shannon said. "But I think a transfer is coming anyway, and I should probably get ready to leave town." She swallowed back the regrets she had about leaving so much unfinished business in Brush Creek. Maybe she'd be transferred somewhere close enough she could commute. Beaverton had two elementary schools, and it was only fifteen minutes down the road. No matter what happened in Shannon's life, she couldn't give up hope.

She still hoped for a resolution for her and Hannah.

She still hoped Grant would text her back, maybe be waiting on her front porch when she got back from her summer road trip.

She still hoped she'd meet a wonderful man and have a family with him.

All the fun and joy of the evening seemed to fizzle, no matter how she tried to hold onto it.

"Are we waiting for someone?" the waiter asked, and Shannon started to say no when her mom said, "Yes."

The waiter nodded, smiled, and left.

"We are?" Shannon locked eyes with her mom. "Who?"

Her mom's neck seemed barely able to hold her head, and it bobbled around like a doll. "Hannah."

Pure surprise mixed with panic—and that blasted hope —darted through Shannon. "Hannah? She's coming here?" She glanced toward the entrance and scanned the restaurant like her sister would appear out of thin air.

"Just for appetizers."

Shannon frowned. "I thought we were eating dinner."

"*You* are." Her mom smiled and shook her head. "Don't ask questions. Just go with the flow tonight."

"What flow?"

"You don't need to be in charge of everything." Her mom gave her a pointed look, which stabbed right through Shannon's already wounded heart.

"I know that."

"Then you can trust that I've arranged a few things with a few people." She picked up her water glass and took a sip. "You're going to sit right there and enjoy the evening."

"But Hannah...." Tears pricked her eyes. She had so much to say and nowhere to start.

And then she didn't have any time, because someone said, "Hey, Mom. Shannon."

She looked up and found her beautiful, blonde sister

standing at the end of the table. She'd cut her hair into a cute A-line that suited her face, and she carried a purse Shannon would've picked out for her. Shannon found she didn't need words, didn't need to think.

She leapt to her feet and embraced her sister, letting the tears flow down her face and ruin her perfect makeup. In public. She didn't care. Her sister was here.

She leaned back and looked at Hannah, holding her at arm's length. "I'm so sorry. I tried to explain everything. I called and texted. And—"

"I know." Hannah's eyes shone with unshed tears too. "You have nothing to be sorry about." She smiled, but it was timid and hesitant. "You guys didn't order without me, did you? Because I love the potato chip encrusted onion rings here."

Hannah slid into the booth next to their mother, and Shannon half stumbled, half sat back on the bench. She couldn't believe what was happening. "Did Mom ask you to come?" She glanced at her mom, in complete shock that she could hide such a massive surprise.

A smile—a true, genuine smile—spread Hannah's lips. "No."

Confusion riddled Shannon's whole soul. "Then—who?"

"A man named Grant Ford," Hannah said.

CHAPTER 14

Grant had been to Georgia a few times while he traveled with the rodeo, but he'd never really had time to explore the city, sample the food, suffocate in the humidity. Okay, well, the last part wasn't true. Every time he'd come to Atlanta, he'd felt like he was drinking the air.

He paced in his hotel room, eight-thirty still an hour away. Still, he wanted to leave now and spy on Shannon and her family. Hannah had arranged everything, and she should've arrived at the restaurant by now. Grant had wanted to give Shannon the best surprise ever, and it had taken almost a month, dozens and dozens of phone calls, and a fair share of begging to get Hannah to meet with him.

Once she had, though, the iciness he'd felt in her exchanges had melted away, and she'd finally admitted that Shannon had been right about Hannah's ex. He hadn't gotten all the details, but the gist was that Hannah had tracked Steven down and found him with another woman. He'd admitted to her that he'd come on to Shannon.

Grant had offered to meet up with Shannon in the morning, but Hannah had insisted he come to the restaurant tonight. She didn't want more than an hour with Shannon, and Hannah suspected her sister would want to see Grant that very night.

He swallowed, the hope that she'd accept his surprise and his apology and they could pick up where they'd left off almost choking him.

By the time he parked, his only thought centered on running away. Turning his back on this city, and that woman, and finding another ranch in another state.

Then he thought of Shannon, and how he wanted her in his life. He wanted to see where things could go and maybe, just maybe, if she wanted to be a Brush Creek Ranch wife. At eight-twenty-nine, he got out of the truck and straightened his tie and then his cowboy hat.

His legs felt like someone had turned them into wood, but somehow he managed to get through the door. He saw Shannon immediately, off to the right, sitting in a booth across from Hannah and an older version of both girls.

Grant sucked in a breath and held it. Shannon looked as gorgeous as ever, and he couldn't believe he'd been so blind. So wrapped up inside his own head. So prideful and unwilling to see beyond his past.

Please soften Shannon's heart, he prayed. He'd been praying for clarity for weeks, and the answers he'd received had opened doors for him he hadn't even known existed.

He crossed toward her, and she lifted her head when he was halfway to her table. Shock showed plainly on her face, and with every step he took, the more clearly he could see that she'd been crying.

She stood to meet him, and he chuckled nervously. "Surprise," he said, the word sticking in his throat.

She smiled but sobbed and threw herself into his arms. He closed his eyes, relieved to be holding her again.

"We'll catch up tomorrow," Hannah said, sliding out of the booth. Her mom followed, and her blue eyes saw everything.

She paused next to Grant. "Nice to meet you. I hope you'll stop by tomorrow so we can get to know each other."

"Yes, ma'am," he said with a tip of his hat.

She dipped her chin and left with Hannah, leaving Shannon alone with Grant. "You haven't eaten, have you?"

"My sister wouldn't let me order, and I could barely eat anything once I learned you were here."

"So you aren't mad." He slid onto the bench where Hannah had been sitting, and Shannon sat next to him. He took her hand in his. "Are you mad?"

She shook her head, her eyes welling with tears. "I was at first, but not at you."

Grant's heart somersaulted. "At yourself?"

"I can be intense," she said. "I know that."

"My idiocy had nothing to do with you." He squeezed her hand as the waiter arrived with two plates of food.

"Who had the bacon cheeseburger?"

Grant liked cheeseburgers so he indicated himself.

"And the chicken parm."

"That's what I would've ordered," Shannon said. The waiter put down their food and left. Grant spied Hannah loitering near the hostess station, and he nodded toward her. Shannon followed his gaze, and Hannah smiled before she ducked out the door.

"Good surprise?" Grant asked.

"You'll never be able to top it." Shannon picked up her fork. "And I don't deserve it."

"Sure you do." He nudged her with his shoulder. "You deserve the best."

"Does that include you?" She spun spaghetti around and around on her fork, her eyes on her plate but her interest sky-high.

"I hope so," he said. "I'm sorry about what happened. I —" He cleared his throat. "I got scared."

"Of me?"

Grant wanted everything on the table. "I'm not scared of you, Shannon. I'm scared of being good enough for you. I'm scared of not having you in my life. I was scared I'd fallen in love with you too fast. I was—I am—scared of *us*."

"But you want for there to be an us, right?" She raised those beautiful eyes to his, and Grant leaned toward her. He didn't need to eat. He didn't need to breathe. He only needed to kiss Shannon. Now.

"I definitely want there to be an us," he whispered. She smiled and he leaned in further. She closed the distance between them, and this kiss felt like it reinvented him yet again. Like he'd never be the same Grant Ford again.

And that was okay with him.

CHAPTER 15

Shannon could hardly believe that Grant was here. In Atlanta. *Here.*

"So Hannah wouldn't tell me, but how did you get her to agree to talk to me again?"

Grant nearly slopped his soda down the front of his shirt. "She didn't tell you?"

Shannon knew better than to think everything would magically resolve itself in a mere hour-long conversation with her sister. But she didn't like Grant's reaction.

"No, she didn't say."

Grant shifted in his seat. "Well, you should probably ask her."

Frustration coursed through her. "Do you think she'll tell me if I call her?"

"She's your sister. I barely know her."

"How did you get her number?"

He squirmed again. The man seriously had ants in his pants. "You know how people say there's only six degrees of separation between people?"

"Yeah," Shannon said slowly.

"Well, I know a cowboy from my rodeo days who's based here in Atlanta. I talked to him, who talked to his sister, who has a friend who works at the university...."

"My mom works at the university."

Grant grinned. "It only took about a week."

"And you just called her."

"Called her right up, out of the blue."

Shannon felt like squirming but held still. "Was she nice?"

"She hung up on me."

She gaped at him, her eyes wide.

"Three times." Grant chuckled. "I see why you're so stubborn. Is that from your mom or your dad?"

"Both," Shannon muttered, which caused Grant to laugh. He swung his arm around her shoulder and tucked her into his side as he dipped a French fry in ketchup.

"I'm so glad to be here," he murmured. The husky, warm tone of his voice, and the pine-scented nature of his skin drove Shannon's pulse to pounding. She turned into him and kissed him, enjoying the saltiness on his lips and the way he seemed to be hers when they touched.

He pulled away sooner than she would've liked, a dark red stain creeping up his neck. "We should eat and then...go somewhere more private."

Shannon tossed her hair over her shoulder and laughed. "Right. Eating now. Kissing later."

———

SHANNON DIDN'T LEAVE Atlanta the next morning. Her sister arrived at her mom's house just as Shannon stepped into the kitchen looking for coffee. Hannah had brought Grant with her, as he was staying in a hotel and didn't have a car.

Shannon kissed him hello and then gripped her sister in a tight hug, the kind she used to give after months had passed without any Hannah-time. When she pulled away, she found tears in Hannah's eyes. "You okay?"

"I'm sorry about everything," she said, sniffling.

"You already said that last night."

"I've known for months that you were right."

Shannon paused in her caffeine retrieval. "What do you mean?"

"I mean I followed Steven up to Washington D.C. I told him we could still be together, that I'd visit my family without him. He was...." She shook her head, the tears slipping down her cheeks quickly now. "He was already engaged to someone else. He said we could have a little fun if I wanted, whenever I wanted."

She hung her head. "I asked him if he'd come onto you, and he admitted it."

Shannon's emotions warred. Vindication that she'd been right and Hannah knew it. Horror at the man Hannah had fallen for. Heartache for her sweet sister. She pulled Hannah back into a hug. "When did you find out?"

"Valentine's Day."

Five months. She'd known for *five months*. And Shannon had texted and called plenty of times since Valentine's Day. She swallowed back her rearing anger. She had no idea what Hannah had been through, being only months away from marrying who she thought was the man of her dreams and then learning the awful truth about him.

"I'm sorry," Shannon said again, her voice foreign to her own ears. "Mom went to get pastries, so we can carbo-load and talk about it."

"No, that won't work," Grant said.

Shannon turned toward him as she released her sister. He extended a mug toward her. "Why not?"

"Your mother promised me a fun-filled day of all the tourist sites." He calmly sipped his coffee. "Said you've never been to them either. I've seen you when you carbo-load." He clucked his tongue, the teasing sparkle in his eye so bright it almost blinded her. "Another flaw, I suppose."

Shannon blinked at him. Hannah burst into laughter. Grant just stood there, all handsome and twinkly, sipping his coffee.

"You are so lucky to have him," Hannah said as she stepped into the kitchen. She poured herself a cup of coffee and leaned against the counter.

"I suppose," Shannon said in the same tone he'd used about her flaws. He reached for her and held her close.

"I love you," he whispered. "Flaws and all."

She froze in his embrace. She'd never heard those three little words from a man before. Certainly not in such a throaty whisper. She tipped her head back and locked eyes with him. "You do?"

"Mm." He smiled at her, the wattage of it off the charts and lighting the whole room. "So, Atlanta touristy attractions then?" he said in a loud voice.

"I'm in," Hannah said from the kitchen.

Shannon nodded, because she couldn't quite get her voice to work. If she could, she wanted to say *I love you too.*

EIGHT MONTHS LATER:

Good luck this morning.

Shannon glanced at the text and smiled. Grant always remembered the things she was most worried about. Of course, she'd talked and talked and talked about this meeting with her supervisor. Transfers always came through in late February or early March, and she'd been expecting one for a full year.

She twirled the diamond she wore on her left ring finger, anxious to finally have the complete set soldered together. She'd have to be married for that to happen, and the wedding sat five weeks away.

She inhaled, parked her car, and fired off a text to Grant. She didn't tell him about her nerves. He already knew, as he'd held her last night on his couch and told her that they'd be fine no matter what happened. He could leave Brush Creek Ranch if he had to.

But she didn't want him to do that. If anything, she wanted to move up to the ranch, quit her job, and start having his kids. Over the past eight months as she went up to the horse ranch more and more often, she'd fallen in love with the scenery, his cabin, and all the people who lived up there. The ranch boasted its own community, with families, children, dogs and cats, and the most beautiful country God could create.

Shannon wanted a piece of that for herself. They'd talked about having a family as soon as possible after their wedding. They'd talked about possibly moving. They'd talked about his debts—which he'd finished paying off two months ago. Everything was in place; all her dreams were about to come true.

She just needed to get through this meeting.

She straightened her jacket once she'd gotten out of the car. Pressed her lips together to make sure her lipstick was still pigmented. Adjusted her jewelry. All the pieces were in place. She marched into her supervisor's office and said, "Good morning, John."

"Ah, Shannon. Come in. Sit down." The man half stood and shook her hand across his desk before she sat. He smiled at her. "Almost ready for the wedding?"

Shannon returned the grin. "Almost."

"How long now?"

"Five weeks."

She was friendly with John, but their relationship had always revolved around business. "Transfers are in." He drew a stack of folders toward him, the small talk clearly over. "I know you've been expecting one."

Everything in Shannon felt wrong. "I have." Her voice sounded like she'd swallowed broken glass.

John opened the top folder, and she put her hand on the desk. He glanced at her, curiosity in his expression. "Shannon?"

"Whatever it is, I don't want it." Her heart raced like it was a car in the Indianapolis 500.

"You don't want it?" John frowned at her. "You can't stay at Brush Creek Elementary."

"I don't want to."

He settled back into his chair. "Then what?"

Her lungs squeezed as they worked to bring in oxygen. "John, I'm going to retire."

His eyebrows surged toward his hairline. "Retire?"

"I have twelve years with the district. I looked up the policy. I can retire with ten."

"You'll get almost no benefit." He seemed genuinely concerned.

Shannon thought of Grant, the horse ranch, the three dogs they owned between them and how they frolicked through the fields. "I'll get what I earned," she said. "This is what I want."

He didn't move a muscle, his hazel eyes fixed on hers. "Are you sure?"

Shannon's pulse quieted. She settled back into her chair too, as calm as she'd ever been. "I am absolutely sure."

She hadn't talked about this particular scenario with Grant, but such a sense of calm cascaded over her that she knew she'd made the right decision. For her. For him. For *them*.

Thank you, she thought, a smile dressing her lips. She had never been as happy as she was in that moment. She leapt to her feet. She needed to talk to Grant, now. "Are we finished?"

John reached for his phone and picked it up. "Sarah, can you get the retirement application for Shannon Sharpe? I'm sending her out now." He sighed and stood. "It's been a pleasure working with you Shannon. Don't be a stranger." He came around the desk and walked her to his office door before he shook her hand.

Shannon practically floated out of the office and out to her car. She itched to call Grant, but she wanted to be with him when she told him, see his eyes light up, feel his hands on her waist as he swung her around and laughed into the chilled blue sky.

A half an hour had passed before she made it to Grant's cabin, and even then he wasn't there. Forced to text him, she said, *Can you talk for a minute?*

He didn't answer right away, and she couldn't wait around in the winter temperatures, so she headed back to her car. Tess stepped out onto her porch and called, "Shannon. You wanna come in?"

Shannon changed directions and entered Tess's cabin. She liked the petite blonde who packed a punch, and she slid her a grateful smile as she stepped into the warmth. "Thanks."

"You're not working today?" Tess closed the door behind her as the scent of chocolate and cinnamon filled Shannon's senses.

"Sort of." Shannon rubbed her hands up and down her arms, glancing into the kitchen to find oatmeal chocolate chip cookies. "How's the wedding cake practice coming?"

"Ohh." Tess exhaled. "I had to take a break from it. I'll get it before April fourth, I swear." She wore a look of anxiety.

Shannon giggled and moved toward the cookies. "I don't even care about the cake."

Tess grinned and joined Shannon in the kitchen. "Yeah, it's just about the man, right?"

"Right. I should just run away to Evanston and get married in City Hall." She bumped Tess with her hip and picked up two cookies. Her phone beeped, and she saw a text from Grant.

Sure. Want me to call you?

Can you come to your cabin? She sent the text and bit into a cookie.

You're at my cabin?

With cookies.

On my way.

"Can I take a couple of these?" She gestured toward the cookies.

"Something going on?"

Shannon couldn't help grinning and grinning. "I quit my job today." She danced toward the front door and escaped before Tess could say anything else.

Grant reacted in exactly the way Shannon had hoped, and she didn't end up going back to the school that afternoon but took to hanging out in the cattle area, her hands stuck in one of Grant's big coats, watching him work. It was the best afternoon of her life.

CHAPTER 16

The sky was the shade of sapphires when Grant exited his cabin on his wedding day. The air smelled like fresh rain and pollen, and he couldn't remember a day as glorious as this one. He shouldered his garment bag and tossed it onto the bench seat next to him.

"Are you ready?"

The sound of Landon's voice made Grant turn. "Very ready." It had been a very long ten months since he'd gotten back together with Shannon. Well, not long in a bad way. He enjoyed spending time with her, holding her, listening to her talk, supporting her through her workload at school.

But he really wanted her on the ranch full time. He wanted to wake up next to her, and kiss her without any of her pieces in place. He couldn't wait for the end of the school year, because it meant she wouldn't have to go back, something he knew she desperately wanted. He'd already started planning the last day of school surprise, and he was glad he wouldn't have to do another one.

"I'm happy for you." Landon stepped toward him and

man-clapped him on the back before pulling him into a proper hug. "You deserve her."

How he knew exactly what to say, Grant didn't know. But Landon usually did. "Are you coming with me?"

"That was the plan."

"Get in, then. I don't want to be late to my own wedding." Grant drummed his thumbs against the steering wheel on the way down the canyon, and he parked in the nearest possible spot to the entrance of the red brick church. Shannon's car was already there, and his heart leapt once, twice, three times.

He was marrying Shannon Sharpe today. A smile took over his whole face, and he whistled as he entered the church. An hour later, he was on the edge of impatience and about to stride down the hall to the bride's room and demand to know what was taking Shannon so long.

Landon guided him to the front of the chapel, where the preacher stood at the altar. Family and friends had already gathered, including Hannah and Shannon's mother, who had been in town for a week already. Grant turned away from everyone, his stomach churning. He met Pastor Peters' eyes, and the kindness shining there calmed him.

"I just met with her," he said. "She'll be out any minute." The pastor smiled. "Are you ready for your bride?"

Grant chuckled, releasing all the nerves. "I don't know, sir. Is one ever ready for a beautiful woman?"

The pastor tipped his head back and laughed, the sound loud and quiet at the same time. "You're a wise man, Grant," Pastor Peters said. He nodded toward the back of the chapel, and Grant spun to find Shannon standing there, every single piece in its exact right place.

His limbs felt like dead weight, and numbness spread outward from his core. Shannon moved forward one agonizingly slow step at a time. Grant thought sure she'd never reach him, and then there she was, slipping her arm into his and beaming at him with the force of the sun.

He thought he should've said something about how beautiful she was, how the dress she wore fit her like a glove and was simply stunning, but his tongue felt huge inside his mouth. Her demeanor dimmed, and a question entered her eyes.

Grant thawed and grinned at her. "I'm so happy."

Her brightness returned, and she stretched up and kissed his cheek. "Me too."

"No kissing until after the ceremony," Pastor Peters chided, and a low laugh ran through the crowd.

"We are gathered here this morning to unite this man and this woman in holy matrimony." The pastor gave his speech, and Grant enjoyed his words as he spoke about loving and cherishing each other.

When he said, "There will be hard times," Grant stood a little taller. He could weather stormy situations. Shannon's fingers tightened in his.

"I advise you to cleave unto one another in those times. Don't rely on outside sources. Find joy and solace at home, and always confide in each other. That's how you'll make it through the tough times on your journey through this life."

With that done, the pastor proceeded to marry them, ending with, "All right, Grant. You can kiss your bride now."

Grant obliged, his smile so huge he almost couldn't form his mouth to Shannon's. She giggled, and so great was her joy that Grant felt it infect the very air around him. Landon whooped, and the rest of the crowd came alive too.

Grant laughed then, and ducked down the aisle and out of the church amidst a flurry of bubbles that Shannon's school kids blew. His truck had been properly smeared with shaving cream and streamers, with his and Shannon's luggage in the back. He helped her inside, making sure the skirts of her dress wouldn't get shut in the door, and then positioned himself behind the wheel.

He looked at Shannon. Leaned over and kissed her. "We did it."

"We sure did."

He started the truck and put it in gear, honking at his cowboy friends and their ranch wives before pulling onto the road that led out of town. "And now, we're going to Hawai'i."

"Seven days on the beach." Shannon scooted over and rested her head on his shoulder. "I love you, Grant."

Gratitude accompanied the grin that sprang to his face. He said, "I love you too, sweetheart," glad he'd taken that chance on the two of them.

Read on for a sneak peek of the first book in the spinoff series, The Fuller Family of Brush Creek, **THE MARINE'S MARRIAGE**. This spinoff series contains 6 more books, each featuring a Fuller Family member!

Sneak Peek! The Marine's Marriage Chapter One

Wren Fuller pushed into the office she ran to the shrill sound of the phone ringing. Already. She sighed, this Monday shaping up to achieve the horrible reputation all Mondays dealt with.

She'd arrived at A Jack of All Trades, the family owned and operated business, fifteen minutes early. Whoever was calling could leave a message. Wren dropped her purse at the desk where she sat and continued through the door to the left so she could put her lunch in the fridge.

It would be nothing short of a miracle if her sisters came in today. They sometimes did after their house-cleaning jobs, but Wren had them pretty well booked today, much to Fabi's disgust. The oldest of the twins, Fabi loved sleeping in as much as the rest of the Fuller clan, Wren included.

But whatever. Wren tucked her hair behind her ear and deposited her brown bag in the fridge. She paused and looked in the mirror to the side of the door that led back to the reception area, trying to make her blonde hair grow longer just by staring at it.

It was in this weird, in-between stage she hated. But she didn't like her hair long either, so she'd cut it. But she didn't have a feminine enough face for a short, pixie cut, so she was growing it back out.

No matter what she did, her hair seemed determined to make her life more difficult.

As she settled into the ergonomic office chair she'd insisted Daddy buy, the phone rang again. Though they still didn't open for another ten minutes, she answered the call with a chirpy, "A Jack of All Trades, it should be a good Monday," and waited for a chuckle or at least half a giggle.

She got silence.

"Hello?" she asked.

"Yes, hello," a man said, his tone the no-nonsense clipped kind. "I need a maid."

"Well, we certainly can help you with that." Wren's four sisters managed to keep their schedules full with the amount of dust and dishes that the townspeople in Brush Creek wanted someone else to take care of. Especially in the summer, when they'd rather go camping, fishing, hiking, or strawberry-picking.

"Let's see," she said, tapping to wake her computer. Sometimes it took an extra few seconds to find the WiFi after being asleep overnight. Thankfully, it fired right up today, and she had the family's online calendar open in less time than it took to inhale and exhale.

"I can get someone out to you next Tuesday."

"Next Tuesday?"

"That's right. It's best if you get on our regular schedule. That way, we'll come at the same time every week, or every two weeks, or once a month. It's—"

"I just need someone once. I can clean my own house."

"Oh." Wren blinked, the man's tone the type that shut down conversations and left no room for argument. "Then I can get you an appointment for next Tuesday." And if he could clean his own house, why had he called her and asked for a maid?

"I need someone today. Is that possible?" He removed the demand from his question. Sort of.

"I'm sorry," she said. "My girls are all on other jobs."

"I just arrived in town," he said. "I just need help for a few hours today, and then I can get my stuff moved in."

"Oh, you're new?" Wren leaned back in the chair and put her shoes on the edge of the desk. "How did you hear about us?" Wren wasn't sure, but she could've sworn he growled.

"Erin at the bakery. And Landon up at the horse farm."

Wren grinned and nodded, though this new stranger to Brush Creek couldn't see her. She pushed the glasses she didn't need to wear higher on her nose. "Some of our best clients."

"I've got to take Octagon up to the horse farm, actually. Then I'd like to move in."

"So you want someone to come right now, this morning?"

"If possible. I'll pay double the rate."

"You don't even know what the rate is." Wren enjoyed this exchange more than she should've. She should tell this guy to find someone else and begin her morning Solitaire game until she had to get some work done for the day.

"Can you send someone or not?"

Wren could send someone...herself. Technically, she could be out of the office for the morning. Any calls that came here would forward to her cell, and she could pocket the extra cash as a tip.

"Give me a few seconds to check with one of my girls." She put the man on hold as he started to protest, a grin flirting with her lips. She wasn't exactly dressed for scrubbing sinks or mopping floors, but she could do it. Heaven knew she'd spent enough time growing up cleaning everything from tack rooms, to trucks, to toilets.

Still, she loved this shirt with the bright purple My Little Pony on it. Bleach would not be kind to it, so she resolved to grab an apron from the closet in the kitchen before she went out on the job.

She pressed the hold button and said, "I can send Wren."

"Great," he said, almost a deadpan.

"Where am I sending her?"

"I'm on Traverse Road?" He spoke the name like a question, but that wasn't the reason Wren's blood turned cold.

"Traverse Road?" she repeated it like a question.

"Yeah. It's the first one after you turn. I guess a family named Hammond used to live here."

"I know it," Wren said, the rundown house flashing through her mind. She straightened, intending to tell him she was Wren and she'd be there in twenty minutes.

"Great. Good-bye." He hung up before Wren could say anything. She tilted her head and stared at the receiver, wondering if the entire call had been a prank. It didn't seem to be. She hung up and exhaled as she stood.

"Good news, Wren," she said. "You can change before you go *next door* and clean the house that should've been knocked down years ago."

———

WREN HADN'T SEEN anyone around the old Hammond place, ever. Her house sat a hundred yards past it, on the same side of the street, and she drove by every morning and every evening. So really, anyone could've come and gone during the day and she wouldn't have known.

She liked to think she would've noticed tire tracks, or something left on the porch, or that one of the fence slats had been nudged slightly out of place. But she hadn't noticed anything.

After she changed and pulled into the driveway, she still didn't see anything that told her someone had purchased this home and planned to live here.

Because it was pure madness. The porch needed to be replaced, as did the railing, the roof, and all the windows. The whole thing needed to be remodeled, and Wren actually worried that her foot would bust through the steps as she climbed them to the front door.

So she'd put on a few pounds. She didn't care. She'd listened to her mom put her value in the number on the scale, and she didn't want her life to be measured in pounds. Maybe she chose nachos when she should've opted for the Caesar salad. But at least she could walk around with a smile on her face.

"Hello?" she called when she noticed the front door gaped open a couple of inches. No one responded, and she caught sight of a scrap of paper taped to the doorframe.

Come on in and get started. I took my horse up to the ranch. Be back later.

Relief rushed through Wren, and she pushed the front door open further. The inside of the house hadn't fared much better than the outside, much to Wren's disappointment. He hadn't given specific instructions for what he wanted cleaned, but it was obvious the kitchen in the back needed a thorough scrub from top to bottom. All the floors needed to be stripped of their dust. And one peek down the hallway showed three bedrooms and a bathroom that all needed a vacuum, a duster, and a whole lot of elbow grease to make them habitable.

"Did he even look at this place before he bought it?" she wondered as she set her bucket of cleaning supplies on the tile in the kitchen. If he had, he would've known he couldn't just move right in.

She started in the kitchen, glad when clear water came from the sink. Wren didn't worry about splashing on the floor, as she'd clean that last.

Two hours—and at least a bucketful of sweat—later, Wren finished the kitchen and living room. She'd emptied her vacuum three times, but the carpet was walkable now. The walls had been wiped down. The light fixtures and shelves had been relieved of their cobwebs. All cupboards and appliances had been scrubbed, and the floor glinted where the sunlight hit it through the back windows. She'd abandoned the bulky black frames she wore to make herself look smarter long ago, as it was too hard to keep pushing them into place as she worked.

She smiled at her progress and wondered when the man would return. It certainly couldn't take that long to drive a horse up to a ranch and drop him off. She moved into the bathroom, secretly hoping he wouldn't return until she was finished. She could bill him.

Bent over the tub, she heard the distinct sound of boots entering the house.

"Hello?" a man called, and he sounded softer, kinder, than he had on the phone.

Wren scraped her bangs off her forehead, cursing her hair for the tenth time that morning as it stuck to the back of her neck. It wasn't quite long enough to pull into a ponytail, and she had the fleeting thought that she'd like to shave every last hair from her head.

She hadn't even made it to her feet when he said, "You call this cleaning?"

Wren faced him and put her hands on her hips. She felt red-faced and sweaty and her guard went right up as she drank in the boxy shape of his shoulders. The deep brown hazel color of his eyes. The way his jaw already held a day's worth of facial hair. It matched the rich brown color of his hair, and Wren suddenly needed a very cold glass of water.

"Yes," she managed to clip between her lips. "I call this cleaning."

"There's dust on the shelves in the living room."

"Impossible," she said. "If that's true, it settled there in the past half-hour."

His eyebrows went up as if he wasn't used to being

questioned. And it was clear he wasn't. "You want me to show you?"

Frustration boiled in her, and though her momma had always taught her to clean until the customer was satisfied, she bent and extracted a duster from the box she'd brought. "I'd rather you just wiped it up." She held the blue duster toward him, satisfied when he looked at her like she'd grown a second head and told him he would too if he touched her.

Who was this man?

Your new next door neighbor, her mind whispered, and Wren regretted her decision to quip at him to do the dusting himself. She started to withdraw her hand, but he reached out and snatched the duster from her, spinning with military-precision on his toe, and marching down the hall.

———

Can Tate and Wren weather a relationship when they're also next-door neighbors? Find out now in **THE MARINE'S MARRIAGE. It's available in paperback and ebook!**

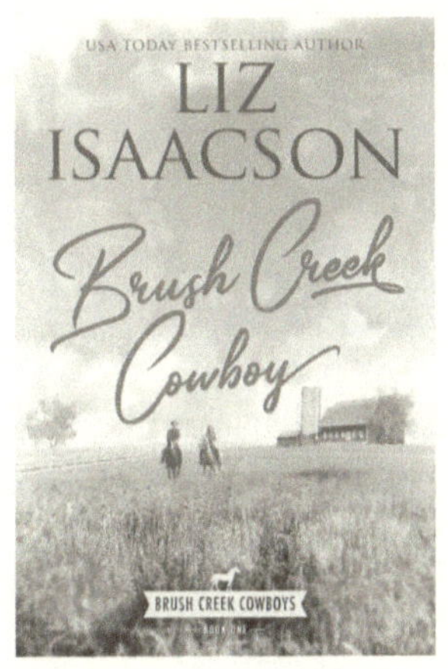

Brush Creek Cowboy (Book 1): Former rodeo champion and cowboy Walker Thompson trains horses at Brush Creek Horse Ranch, where he lives a simple life in his cabin with his ten-year-old son. A widower of six years, he's worked with Tess Wagner, a widow who came to Brush Creek to escape the turmoil of her life to give her seven-year-old son a slower pace of life. But Tess's breast cancer is back...

Walker will have to decide if he'd rather spend even a short time with Tess than not have her in his life at all. Tess wants to feel God's love and power, but can she discover and accept God's will in order to find her happy ending?

The Cowboy's Challenge (Book 2): Cowboy and professional roper Justin Jackman has found solitude at Brush Creek Horse Ranch, preferring his time with the animals he trains over dating. With two failed engagements in his past, he's not really interested in getting his heart stomped on again. But when flirty and fun Renee

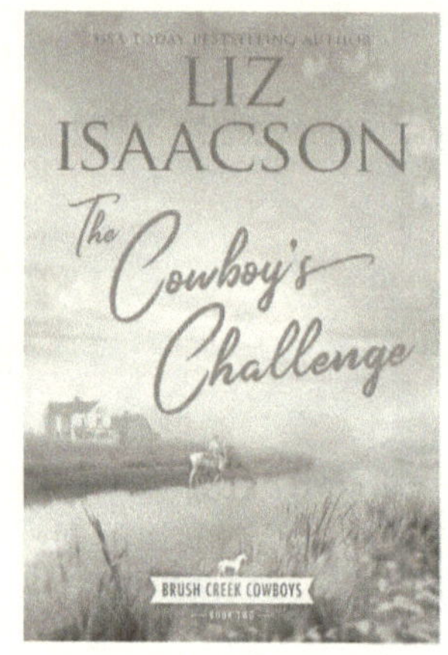

Martin picks him up at a church ice cream bar--on a bet, no less--he finds himself more than just a little interested. His Gen-X attitudes are attractive to her; her Millennial behaviors drive him nuts. Can Justin look past their differences and take a chance on another engagement?

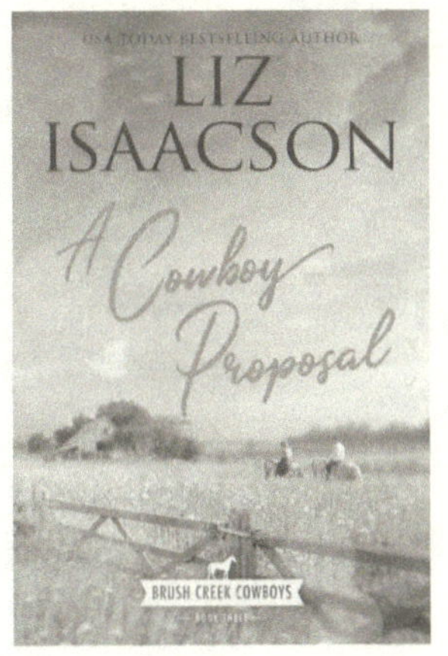

A Cowboy Proposal (Book 3): Ted Caldwell has been a retired bronc rider for years, and he thought he was perfectly happy training horses to buck at Brush Creek Ranch. He was wrong. When he meets April Nox, who comes to the ranch to hide her pregnancy from all her friends back in Jackson Hole, Ted realizes he has a huge family-shaped hole in his life. April is embarrassed, heart-broken, and trying to find her extinguished faith. She's never ridden a horse and wants nothing to do with a cowboy ever again. Can Ted and April create a family of happiness and love from a tragedy?

A New Family for the Cowboy (Book 4): Blake Gibbons oversees all the agriculture at Brush Creek Horse Ranch, sometimes moonlighting as a general contractor. When he meets Erin Shields, new in town, at her aunt's bakery, he's instantly smitten. Erin moved to Brush Creek after a divorce that left her 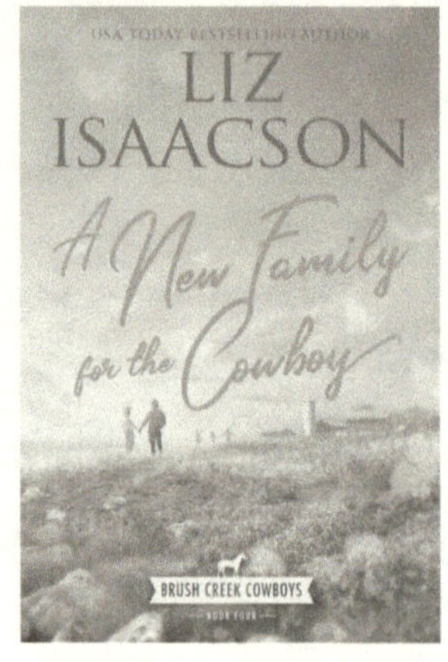 penniless, homeless, and a single mother of three children under age eight. She's nowhere near ready to start dating again, but the longer Blake hangs around the bakery, the more she starts to like him. Can Blake and Erin find a way to blend their lifestyles and become a family?

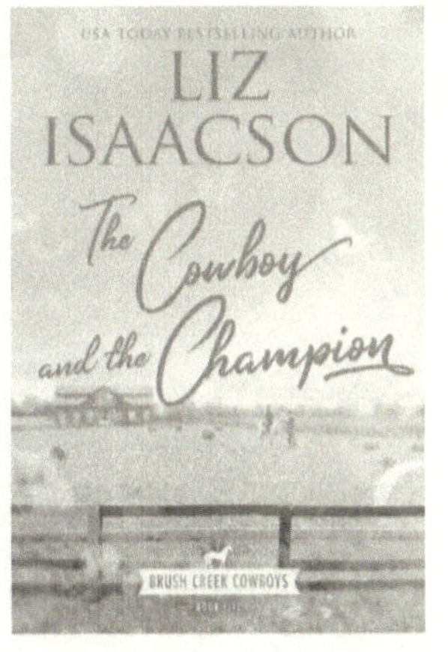

The Cowboy and the Champion (Book 5): Emmett Graves has always had a positive outlook on life. He adores training horses to become barrel racing champions during the day and cuddling with his cat at night. Fresh off her professional rodeo retirement, Molly Brady comes to Brush Creek Horse Ranch as Emmett's protege. He's not thrilled, and she's allergic to cats. Oh, and she'd like to stay cowboy-free, thank you very much. But Emmett's about as cowboy as they come.... Can Emmett and Molly work together without falling in love?

Schooled by the Cowboy (Book 6): Grant Ford spends his days training cattle—when he's not camped out at the elementary school hoping to catch a glimpse of his ex-girl-friend. When principal Shannon Sharpe confronts him and asks him to stay away from the school, the spark between them is instant and hot. Shan-

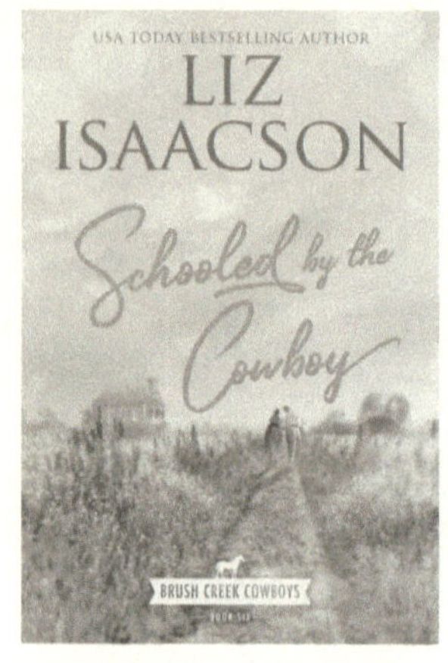

non's expecting a transfer very soon, but she also needs a summer outdoor coordinator—and Grant fits the bill. Just because he's handsome and everything Shannon's ever wanted in a cowboy husband means nothing. Will Grant and Shannon be able to survive the summer or will the Utah heat be too much for them to handle?

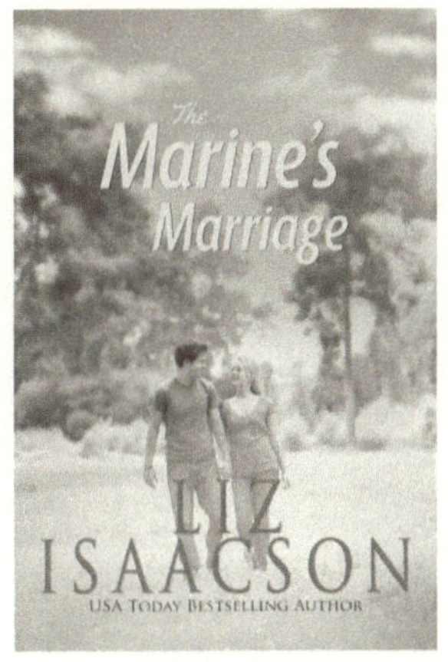

The Marine's Marriage: A Fuller Family Novel - Brush Creek Cowboys Romance (Book 1): Tate Benson can't believe he's come to Nowhere, Utah, to fix up a house that hasn't been inhabited in years. But he has. Because he's retired from the Marines and looking to start a life as a police officer in small-town Brush Creek. Wren Fuller has her hands full most days running her family's company. When Tate calls and demands a maid for that morning, she decides to have the calls forwarded to her cell and go help him out. She didn't know he was moving in next door, and she's completely unprepared for his handsomeness, his kind heart, and his wounded soul. **Can Tate and Wren weather a relationship when they're also next-door neighbors?**

The Firefighter's Fiancé: A Fuller Family Novel - Brush Creek Cowboys Romance (Book 2): Cora Wesley comes to Brush Creek, hoping to get some in-the-wild firefighting training as she prepares to put in her application to be a hotshot. When she meets Brennan Fuller, the spark between them is hot and 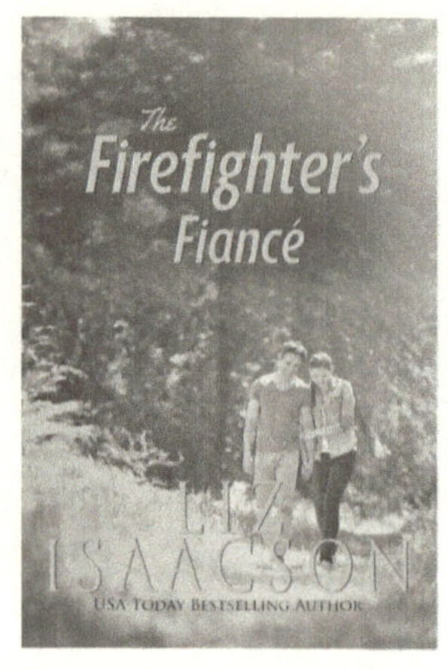 instant. As they get to know each other, her deadline is constantly looming over them, and Brennan starts to wonder if he can break ranks in the family business. He's okay mowing lawns and hanging out with his brothers, but he dreams of being able to go to college and become a landscape architect, but he's just not sure it can be done. **Will Cora and Brennan be able to endure their trials to find true love?**

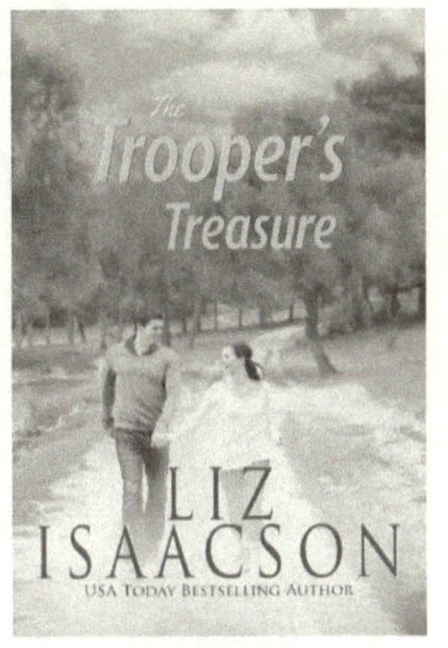

The Trooper's Treasure: A Fuller Family Novel - Brush Creek Cowboys Romance (Book 3): Dawn Fuller has made some mistakes in her life, and she's not proud of the way McDermott Boyd found her off the road one day last year. She's spent a hard year wrestling with her choices and trying to fix them, glad for McDermott's acceptance and friendship. He lost his wife years ago, done his best with his daughter, and now he's ready to move on. **Can McDermott help Dawn find a way past her former mistakes and down a path that leads to love, family, and happiness?**

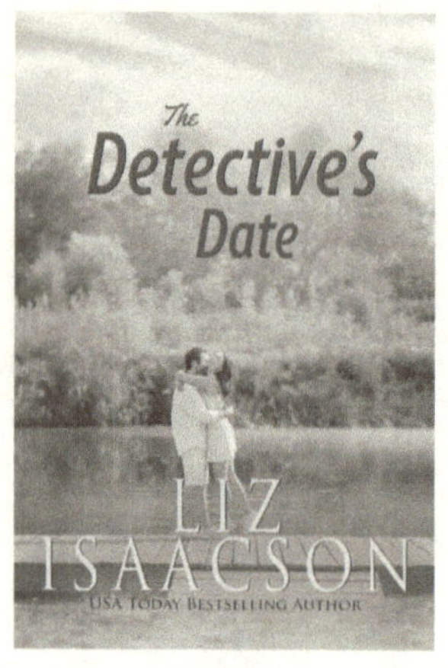

The Detective's Date: A Fuller Family Novel - Brush Creek Cowboys Romance (Book 4): Dahlia Reid is one of the best detectives Brush Creek and the surrounding towns has ever had. She's given up on the idea of marriage—and pleasing her mother—and has dedicated herself fully to her job. Which is great, since one of the most perplexing cases of her career has come to town. Kyler Fuller thinks he's finally ready to move past the woman who ghosted him years ago. He's cut his hair, and he's ready to start dating. Too bad every woman he's been out with is about as interesting as a lamppost—until Dahlia. He finds her beautiful, her quick wit a breath of fresh air, and her intelligence sexy. **Can Kyler and Dahlia use their faith to find a way through the obstacles threatening to keep them apart?**

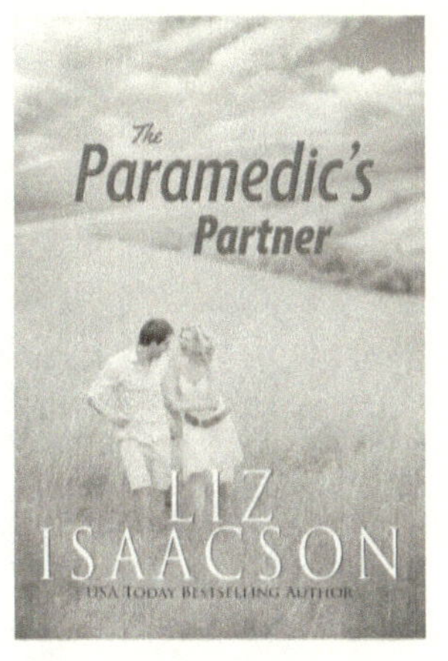

The Paramedic's Partner: A Fuller Family Novel - Brush Creek Cowboys Romance (Book 5): Jazzy Fuller has always been overshadowed by her prettier, more popular twin, Fabiana. Fabi meets paramedic Max Robinson at the park and sets a date with him only to come down with the flu. So she convinces Jazzy to cut her hair and take her place on the date. And the spark between Jazzy and Max is hot and instant...if only he knew she wasn't her sister, Fabi.

Max drives the ambulance for the town of Brush Creek with is partner Ed Moon, and neither of them have been all that lucky in love. Until Max suggests to who he thinks is Fabi that they should double with Ed and Jazzy. They do, and Fabi is smitten with the steady, strong Ed Moon. **As each twin falls further and further in love with their respective paramedic, it becomes obvious they'll need to come clean about the switcheroo sooner rather than later...or risk losing their hearts.**

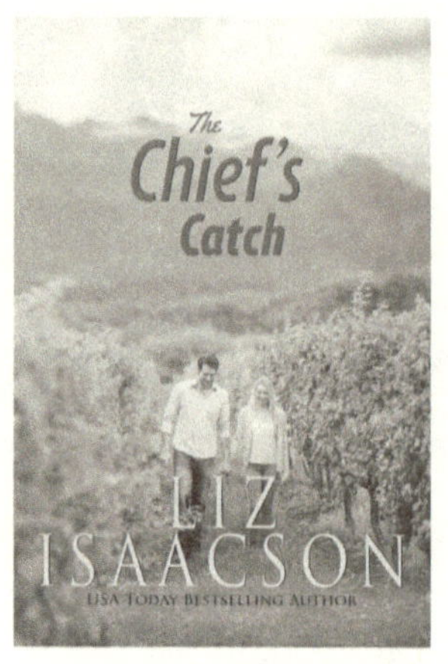

The Chief's Catch: A Fuller Family Novel - Brush Creek Cowboys Romance (Book 6): Berlin Fuller has struck out with the dating scene in Brush Creek more times than she cares to admit. When she makes a deal with her friends that they can choose the next man she goes out with, she didn't dream they'd pick surly Cole Fairbanks, the new Chief of Police.

His friends call him the Beast and challenge him to complete ten dates that summer or give up his bonus check. When Berlin approaches him, stuttering about the deal with her friends and claiming they don't actually have to go out, he's intrigued. As the summer passes, Cole finds himself burning both ends of the candle to keep up with his job and his new relationship. **When he unleashes the Beast one time too many, Berlin will have to decide if she can tame him or if she should walk away.**

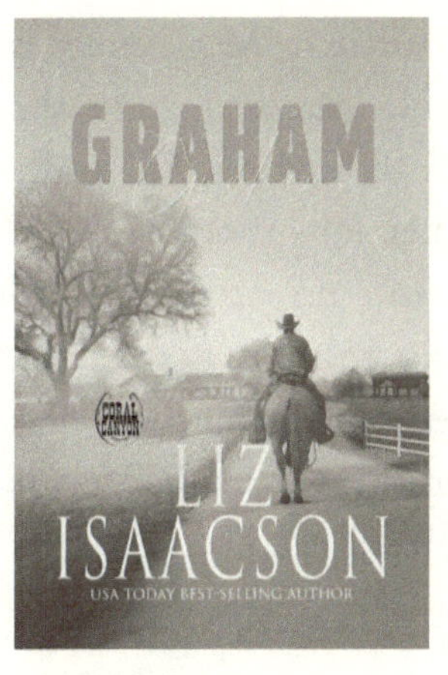

Graham (Book 1): Graham Whittaker returns to Coral Canyon a few days after Christmas—after the death of his father. He takes over the energy company his dad built from the ground up and buys a high-end lodge to live in—only a mile from the home of his once-best friend, Laney McAllister. They were best friends once, but Laney's always entertained feelings for him, and spending so much time with him while they make Christmas memories puts her heart in danger of getting broken again...

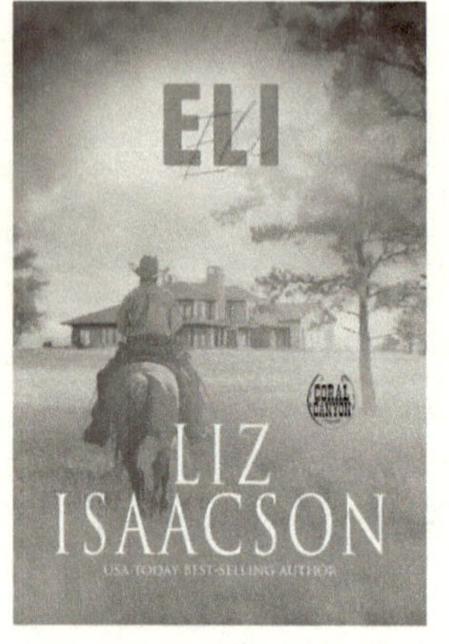

Eli (Book 2): Since the death of his wife a few years ago, Eli Whittaker has been running from one job to another, unable to find somewhere for him and his son to settle. Meg Palmer is Stockton's nanny, and she comes with her boss, Eli, to the lodge, her long-time crush on the man no different in Wyoming than it was on the beach. When she confesses her feelings for him and gets nothing in return, she's crushed, embarrassed, and unsure if she can stay in Coral Canyon for Christmas. Then Eli starts to show some feelings for her too...

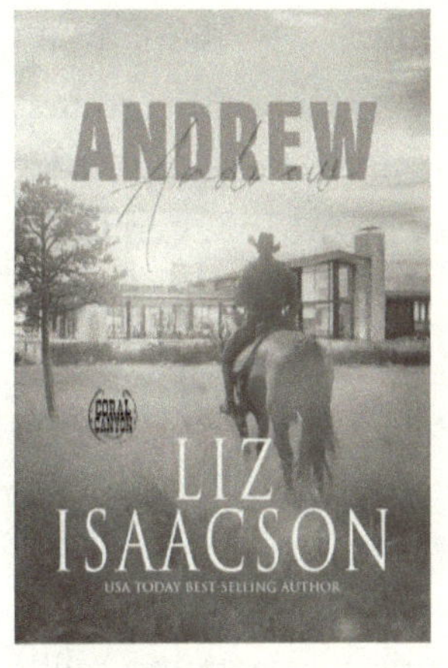

Andrew (Book 3): Andrew Whittaker is the public face for the Whittaker Brothers' family energy company, and with his older brother's robot about to be announced, he needs a press secretary to help him get everything ready and tour the state to make the announcements. When he's hit by a protest sign being carried by the company's biggest opponent, Rebecca Collings, he learns with a few clicks that she has the background they need. He offers her the job of press secretary when she thought she was going to be arrested, and not only because the spark between them in so hot Andrew can't see straight.

Can Becca and Andrew work together and keep their relationship a secret? Or will hearts break in this classic romance retelling reminiscent of *Two Weeks Notice*?

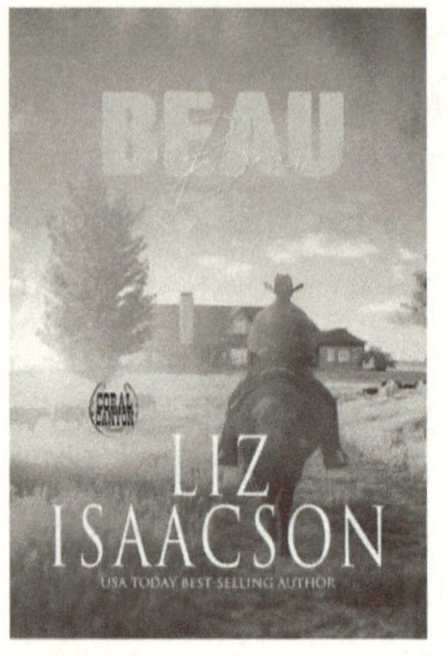

Beau (Book 4): Beau Whittaker has watched his brothers find love one by one, but every attempt he's made has ended in disaster. Lily Everett has been in the spotlight since childhood and has half a dozen platinum records with her two sisters. She's taking a break from the brutal music industry and hiding out in Wyoming while her ex-husband continues to cause trouble for her. When she hears of Beau Whittaker and what he offers his clients, she wants to meet him. Beau is instantly attracted to Lily, but he tried a relationship with his last client that left a scar that still hasn't healed...

Can Lily use the spirit of Christmas to discover what matters most? Will Beau open his heart to the possibility of love with someone so different from him?

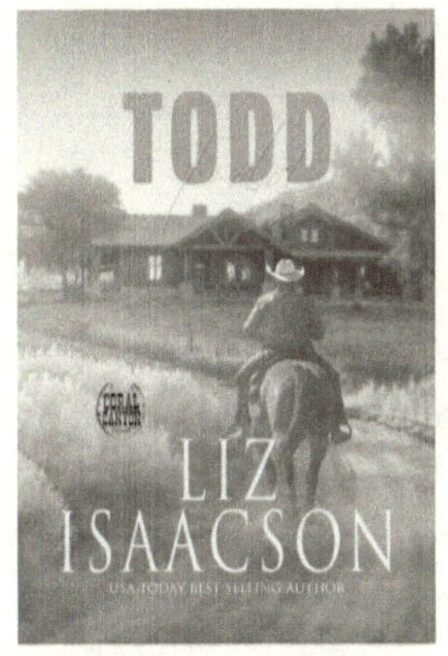

Todd (Book 5): Todd Christopherson has just retired from the professional rodeo circuit and returned to his hometown of Coral Canyon. Problem is, he's got no family there anymore, no land, and no job. Not that he needs a job--he's got plenty of money from his illustrious career riding bulls.

Then Todd gets thrown during a routine horseback ride up the canyon, and his only support as he recovers physically is the beautiful Violet Everett. She's no nurse, but she does the best she can for the handsome cowboy. **Will she lose her heart to the billionaire bull rider? Can Todd trust that God led him to Coral Canyon...and Vi?**

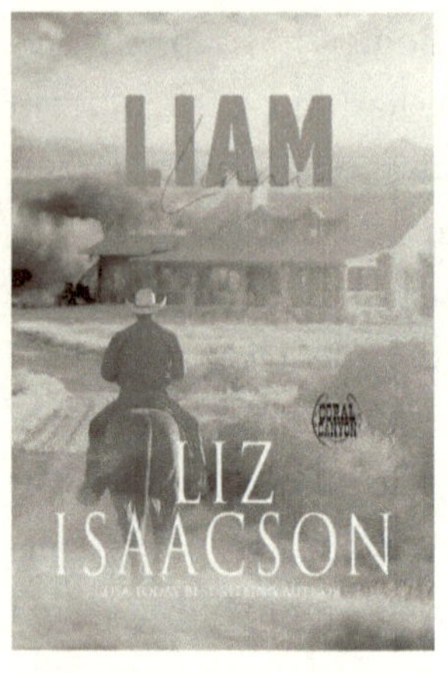

Liam (Book 6): Rose Everett isn't sure what to do with her life now that her country music career is on hold. After all, with both of her sisters in Coral Canyon, and one about to have a baby, they're not making albums anymore.

Liam Murphy has been working for Doctors Without Borders, but he's back in the US now, and looking to start a new clinic in Coral Canyon, where he spent his summers.

When Rose wins a date with Liam in a bachelor auction, their relationship blooms and grows quickly. **Can Liam and Rose find a solution to their problems that doesn't involve one of them leaving Coral Canyon with a broken heart?**

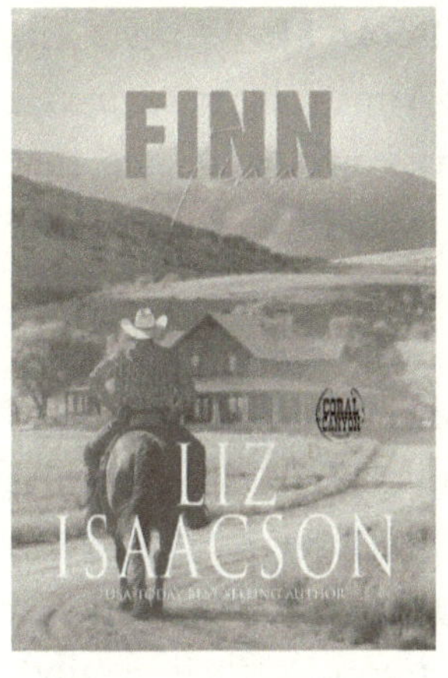

Finn (Book 7): Her sons want her to be happy, but she's too old to be set up on a blind date...isn't she?

Amanda Whittaker has been looking for a second chance at love since the death of her husband several years ago. Finley Barber is a cowboy in every sense of the word. Born and raised on a racehorse farm in Kentucky, he's since moved to Dog Valley and started his own breeding stable for champion horses. He hasn't dated in years, and everything about Amanda makes him nervous.

Will Amanda take the leap of faith required to be with Finn? Or will he become just another boyfriend who doesn't make the cut?

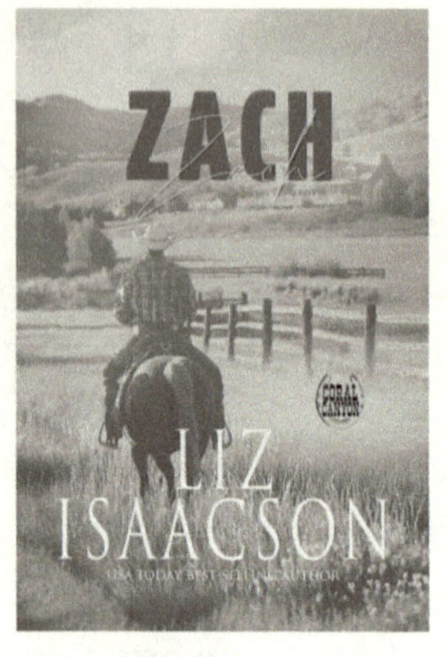

Zach (Book 8): When Celia Abbott-Armstrong runs into a gorgeous cowboy at her best friend's wedding, she decides she's ready to start dating again.

But the cowboy is Zach Zuckerman, and the Zuckermans and Abbotts have been at war for generations.

Can Zach and Celia find a way to reconcile their family's differences so they can have a future together?

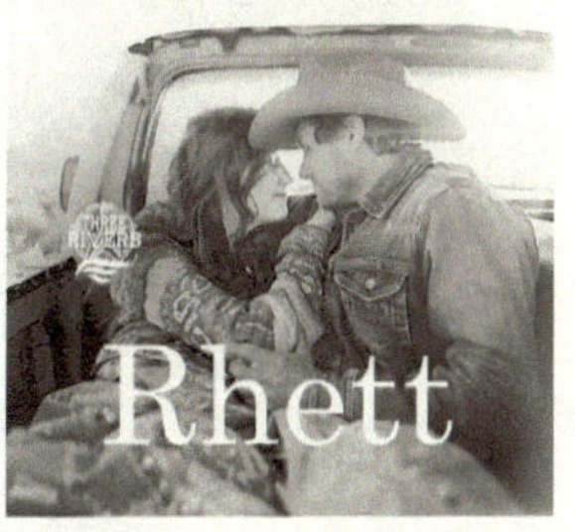

Rhett (Book 1): To save her business, she'll have to risk her heart. She needs a husband to be credible as a matchmaker. He wants to help a neighbor. **Will their fake marriage take them out of the friend zone?**

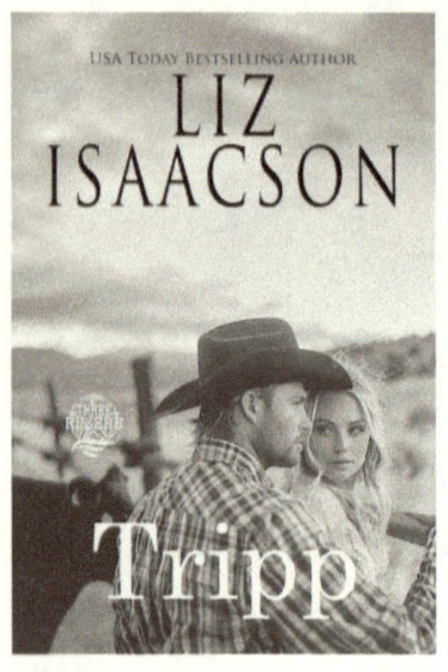

Tripp (Book 2): She needs a husband to keep her son. He's wanted to take their relationship to the next level, but she's always pushing him away. Will their trivial tie take them all the way to happily-ever-after?

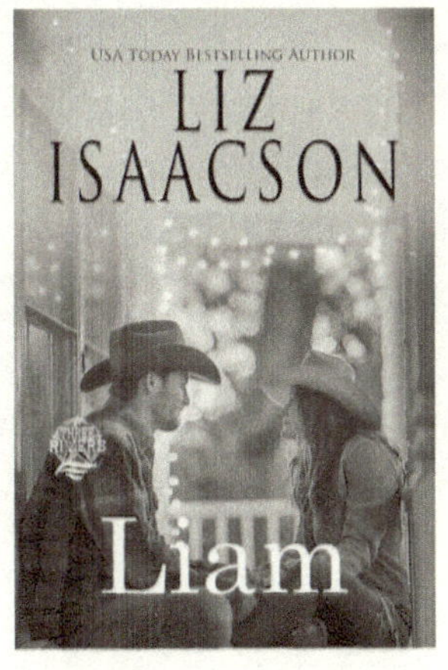

Liam (Book 3): She's desperate to save her ranch. He wants to help her any way he can. Will their invented I-Do open doors that have previously been closed and lead to a happily-ever-after for both of them?

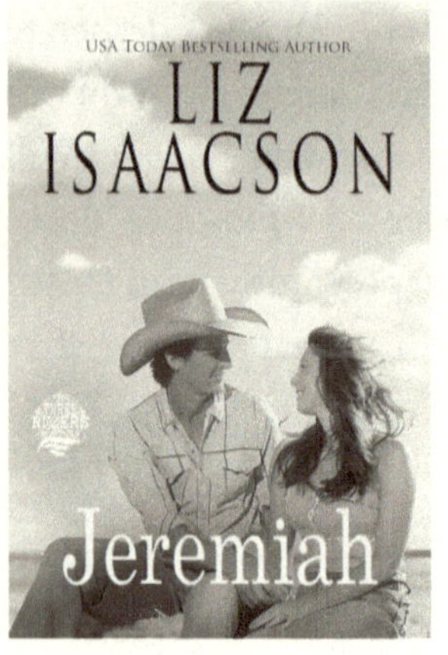

Jeremiah (Book 4): He wants to prove to his brothers that he's not broken. She just wants him. Will a fake marriage heal him or push her further away?

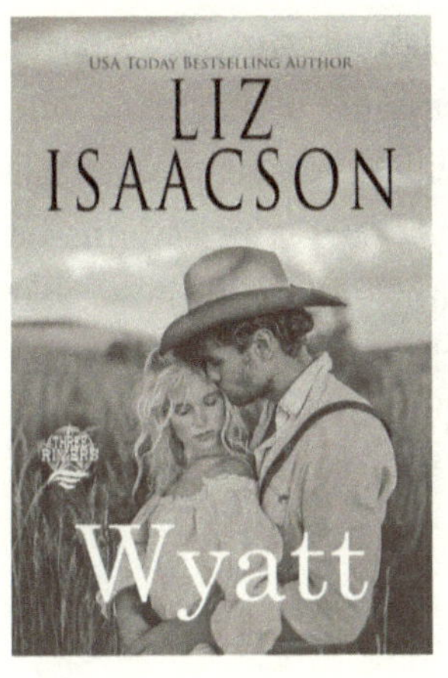

Wyatt (Book 5): To get her inheritance, she needs a husband. He's wanted to fly with her for ages. Can their pretend pledge turn into something real?

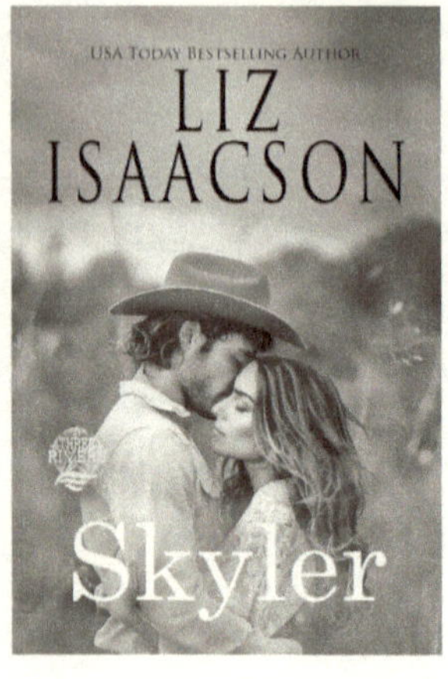

Skyler (Book 6): She needs a new last name to stay in school. He's willing to help a fellow student. Can this wanna-be wife show the playboy that some things should be taken seriously?

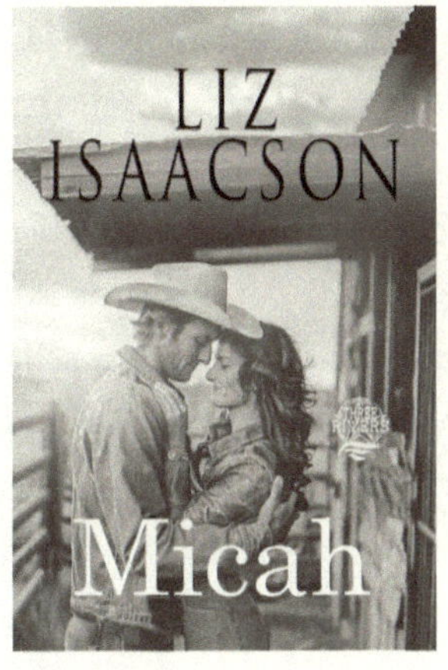

Micah (Book 7): They were just actors auditioning for a play. The marriage was just for the audition – until a clerical error results in a legal marriage. Can these two ex-lovers negotiate this new ground between them and achieve new roles in each other's lives?

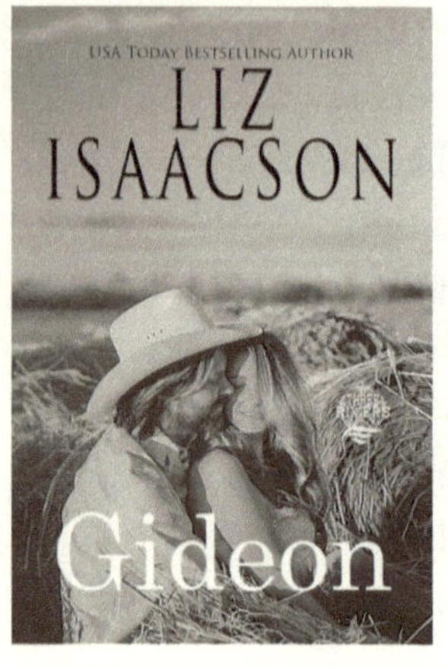 **Gideon (Book 8):** It's 1971, and Gideon Walker is on the cutting edge of all the technology coming out of Texas. He has big dreams and wants to make something of himself. Then he meets Penny Aarons, and everything changes. He only has eyes for her, but she's got plans and dreams of her own...

Read this origin romance for Momma and Daddy from the Seven Sons series today!

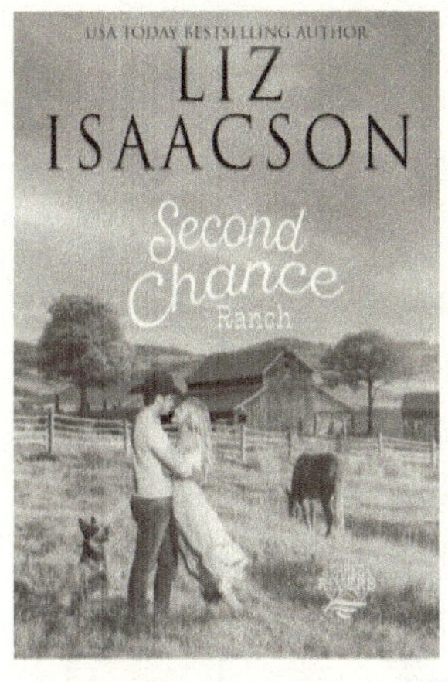 **Second Chance Ranch: A Three Rivers Ranch Romance™ (Book 1):** After his deployment, injured and discharged Major Squire Ackerman returns to Three Rivers Ranch, wanting to forgive Kelly for ignoring him a decade ago. He'd like to provide the stable life she needs, but with old wounds opening and a ranch on the brink of financial collapse, it will take patience and faith to make their second chance possible.

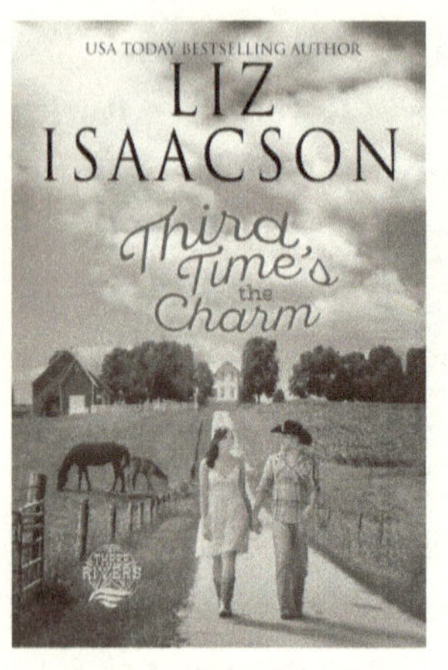

Third Time's the Charm: A Three Rivers Ranch Romance™ (Book 2): First Lieutenant Peter Marshall has a truckload of debt and no way to provide for a family, but Chelsea helps him see past all the obstacles, all the scars. With so many unknowns, can Pete and Chelsea develop the love, acceptance, and faith needed to find their happily ever after?

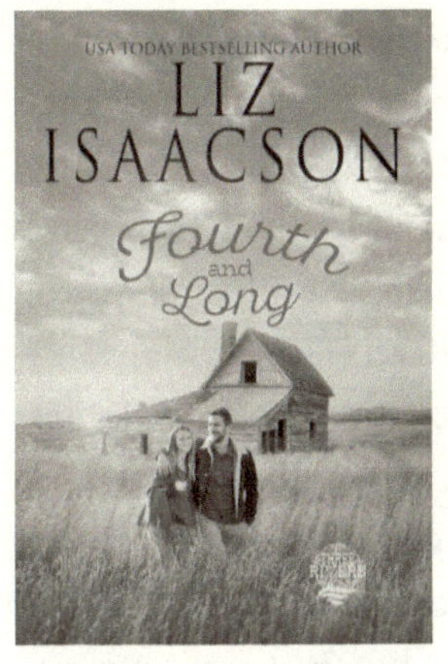

Fourth and Long: A Three Rivers Ranch Romance™ (Book 3): Commander Brett Murphy goes to Three Rivers Ranch to find some rest and relaxation with his Army buddies. Having his ex-wife show up with a seven-year-old she claims is his son is anything but the R&R he craves. Kate needs to make amends, and Brett needs to find forgiveness, but are they too late to find their happily ever after?

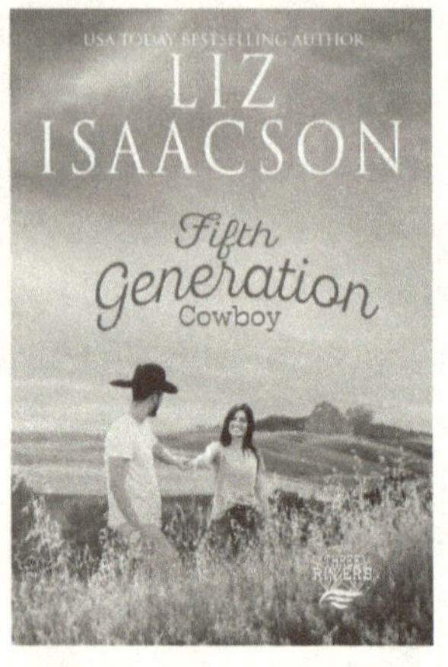

Fifth Generation Cowboy: A Three Rivers Ranch Romance™ (Book 4): Tom Lovell has watched his friends find their true happiness on Three Rivers Ranch, but everywhere he looks, he only sees friends. Rose Reyes has been bringing her daughter out to the ranch for equine therapy for months, but it doesn't seem to be working. Her challenges with Mari are just as frustrating as ever. Could Tom be exactly what Rose needs? Can he remove his friendship blinders and find love with someone who's been right in front of him all this time?

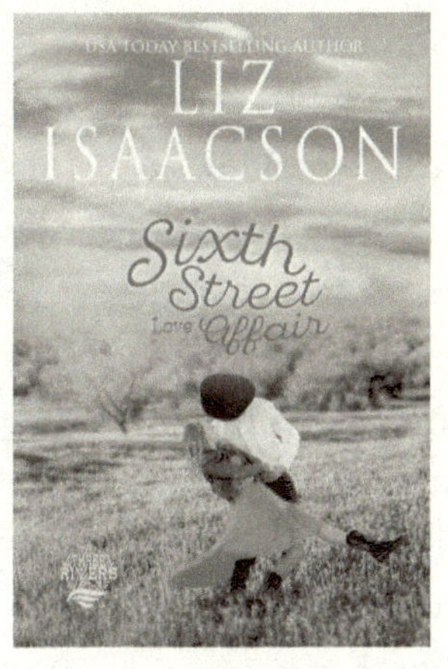

Sixth Street Love Affair: A Three Rivers Ranch Romance™ (Book 5): After losing his wife a few years back, Garth Ahlstrom thinks he's ready for a second chance at love. But Juliette Thompson has a secret that could destroy their budding relationship. Can they find the strength, patience, and faith to make things work?

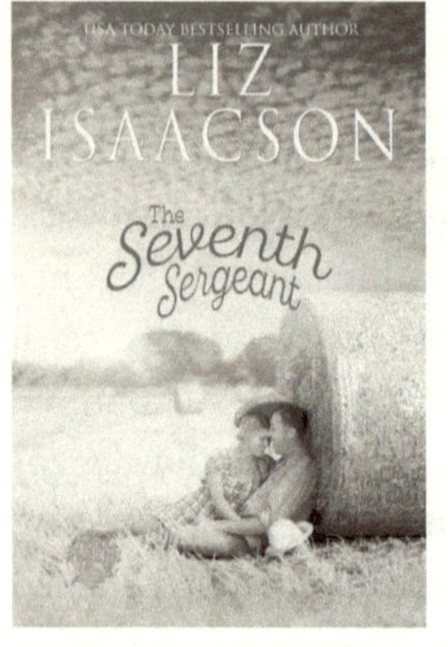

The Seventh Sergeant: A Three Rivers Ranch Romance™ (Book 6): Life has finally started to settle down for Sergeant Reese Sanders after his devastating injury overseas. Discharged from the Army and now with a good job at Courage Reins, he's finally found happiness—until a horrific fall puts him right back where he was years ago: Injured and depressed. Carly Watters, Reese's new veteran care coordinator, dislikes small towns almost as much as she loathes cowboys. But she finds herself faced with both when she gets assigned to Reese's case. Do they have the humility and faith to make their relationship more than professional?

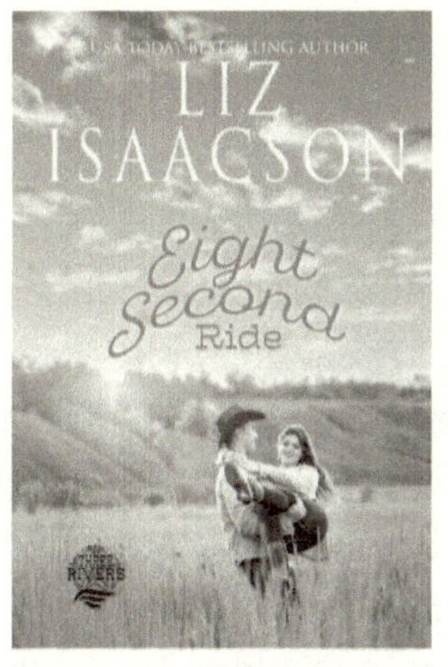

Eight Second Ride: A Three Rivers Ranch Romance™ (Book 7): Ethan Greene loves his work at Three Rivers Ranch, but he can't seem to find the right woman to settle down with. When sassy yet vulnerable Brynn Bowman shows up at the ranch to recruit him back to the rodeo circuit, he takes a different approach with the barrel racing champion. His patience and newfound faith pay off when a friendship--and more--starts with Brynn. But she wants out of the rodeo circuit right when Ethan wants to rejoin. Can they find the path God wants them to take and still stay together?

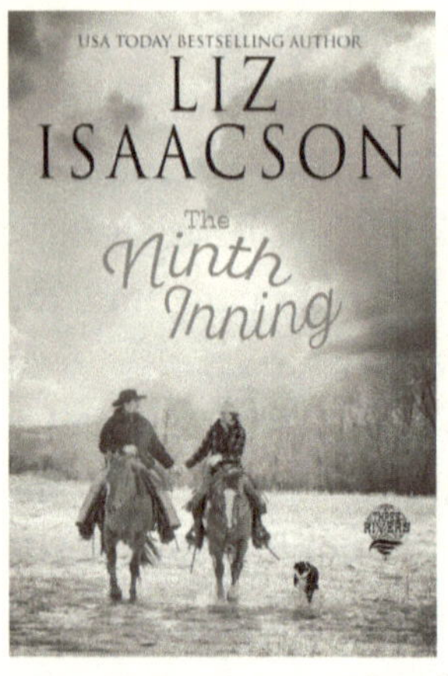

The Ninth Inning: A Three Rivers Ranch Romance™ (Book 8): The Christmas season has never felt like such a burden to boutique owner Andrea Larsen. But with Mama gone and the holidays upon her, Andy finds herself wishing she hadn't been so quick to judge her former boyfriend, cowboy Lawrence Collins. Well, Lawrence hasn't forgotten about Andy either, and he devises a plan to get her out to the ranch so they can reconnect. Do they have the faith and humility to patch things up and start a new relationship?

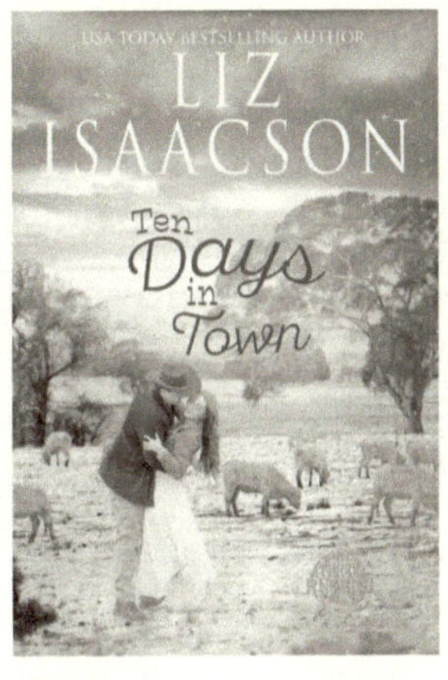

Ten Days in Town: A Three Rivers Ranch Romance™ (Book 9): Sandy Keller is tired of the dating scene in Three Rivers. Though she owns the pancake house, she's looking for a fresh start, which means an escape from the town where she grew up. When her older brother's best friend, Tad Jorgensen, comes to town for the holidays, it is a balm to his weary soul. A helicopter tour guide who experienced a near-death experience, he's looking to start over too--but in Three Rivers. Can Sandy and Tad navigate their troubles to find the path God wants them to take--and discover true love--in only ten days?

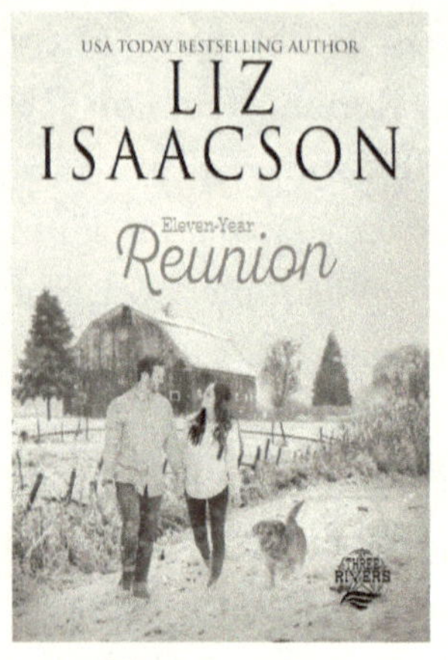

Eleven Year Reunion: A Three Rivers Ranch Romance™ (Book 10): Pastry chef extraordinaire, Grace Lewis has moved to Three Rivers to help Heidi Ackerman open a bakery in Three Rivers. Grace relishes the idea of starting over in a town where no one knows about her failed cupcakery. She doesn't expect to run into her old high school boyfriend, Jonathan Carver. A carpenter working at Three Rivers Ranch, Jon's in town against his will. But with Grace now on the scene, Jon's thinking life in Three Rivers is suddenly looking up. But with her focus on baking and his disdain for small towns, can they make their eleven year reunion stick?

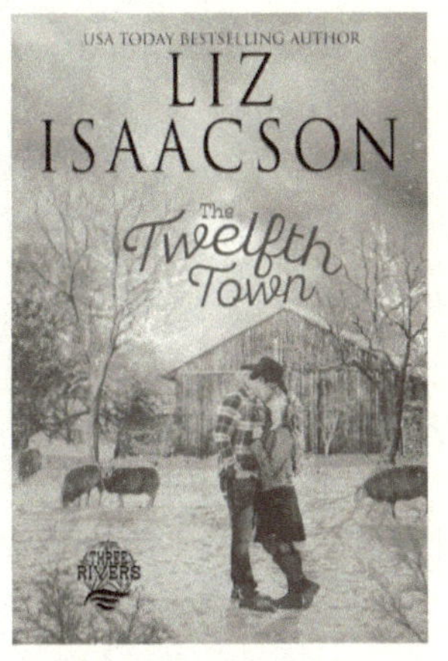

The Twelfth Town: A Three Rivers Ranch Romance™ (Book 11): Newscaster Taryn Tucker has had enough of life on-screen. She's bounced from town to town before arriving in Three Rivers, completely alone and completely anonymous-- just the way she now likes it. She takes a job cleaning at Three Rivers Ranch, hoping for a chance to figure out who she is and where God wants her. When she meets happy-go-lucky cowhand Kenny Stockton, she doesn't expect sparks to fly. Kenny's always been "the best friend" for his female friends, but the pull between him and Taryn can't be denied. Will they have the courage and faith necessary to make their opposite worlds mesh?

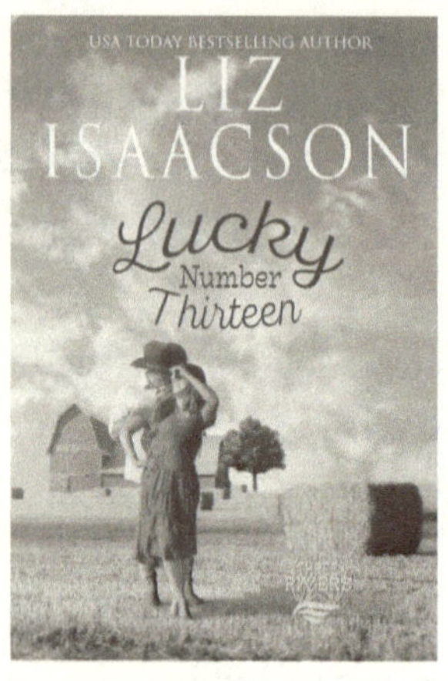

Lucky Number Thirteen: A Three Rivers Ranch Romance™ (Book 12): Tanner Wolf, a rodeo champion ten times over, is excited to be riding in Three Rivers for the first time since he left his philandering ways and found religion. Seeing his old friends Ethan and Brynn is therapuetic--until a terrible accident lands him in the hospital. With his rodeo career over, Tanner thinks maybe he'll stay in town--and it's not just because his nurse, Summer Hamblin, is the prettiest woman he's ever met. But Summer's the queen of first dates, and as she looks for a way to make a relationship with the transient rodeo star work Summer's not sure she has the fortitude to go on a second date. Can they find love among the tragedy?

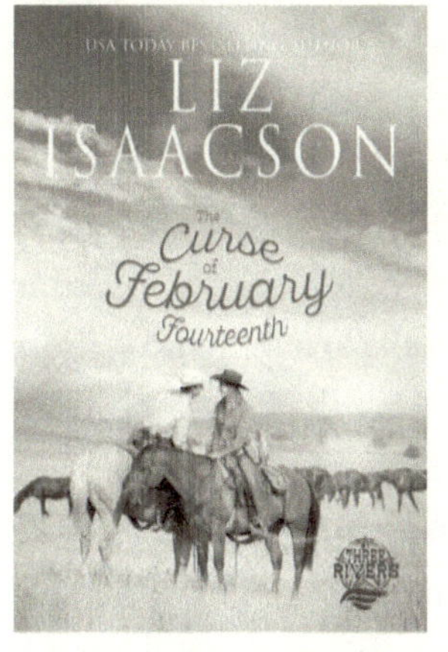

The Curse of February Four-teenth: A Three Rivers Ranch Romance™ (Book 13): Cal Hodgkins, cowboy veterinarian at Bowman's Breeds, isn't planning to meet anyone at the masked dance in small-town Three Rivers. He just wants to get his bachelor friends off his back and sit on the sidelines to drink his punch. But when he sees a woman dressed in gorgeous butterfly wings and cowgirl boots with blue stitching, he's smitten. Too bad she runs away from the dance before he can get her name, leaving only her boot behind...

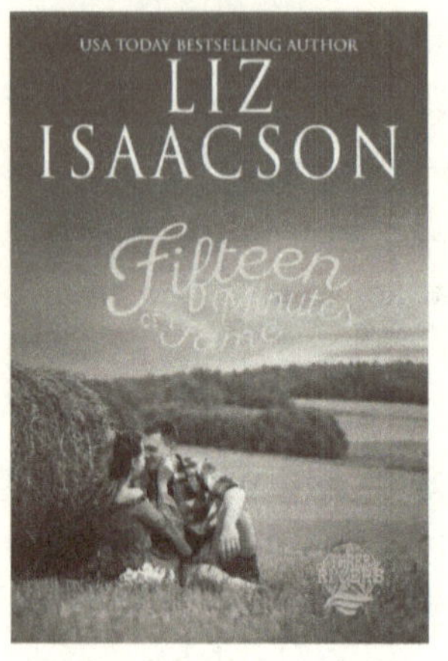

Fifteen Minutes of Fame: A Three Rivers Ranch Romance™ (Book 14): Navy Richards is thirty-five years of tired—tired of dating the same men, working a demanding job, and getting her heart broken over and over again. Her aunt has always spoken highly of the matchmaker in Three Rivers, Texas, so she takes a six-month sabbatical from her high-stress job as a pediatric nurse, hops on a bus, and meets with the matchmaker. Then she meets Gavin Redd. He's handsome, he's hardworking, and he's a cowboy. But is he an Aquarius too? Navy's not making a move until she knows for sure...

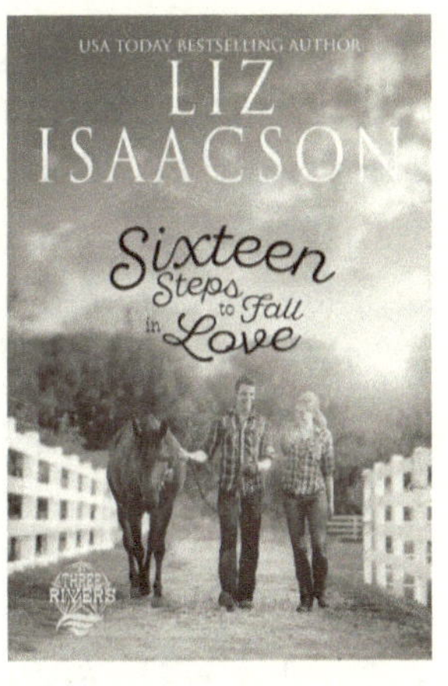

Sixteen Steps to Fall in Love: A Three Rivers Ranch Romance™ (Book 15): A chance encounter at a dog park sheds new light on the tall, talented Boone that Nicole can't ignore. As they get to know each other better and start to dig into each other's past, Nicole is the one who wants to run. This time from her growing admiration and attachment to Boone. From her aging parents. From herself.

But Boone feels the attraction between them too, and he decides he's tired of running and ready to make Three Rivers his permanent home. **Can Boone and Nicole use their faith to overcome their differences and find a happily-ever-after together?**

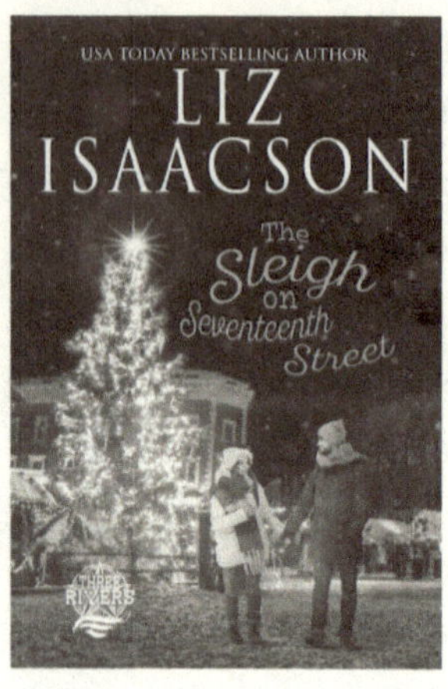

The Sleigh on Seventeenth Street: A Three Rivers Ranch Romance™ (Book 16): A cowboy with skills as an electrician tries a relationship with a down-on-her luck plumber. Can Dylan and Camila make water and electricity play nicely together this Christmas season? Or will they get shocked as they try to make their relationship work?

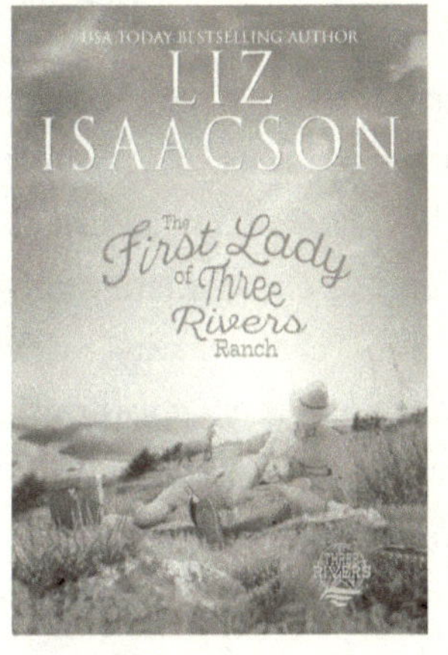

The First Lady of Three Rivers Ranch: A Three Rivers Ranch Romance™ (Book 17): Heidi Duffin has been dreaming about opening her own bakery since she was thirteen years old. She scrimped and saved for years to afford baking and pastry school in San Francisco. And now she only has one year left before she's a certified pastry chef. Frank Ackerman's father has recently retired, and he's taken over the largest cattle ranch in the Texas Panhandle. A horseman through and through, he's also nearing thirty-one and looking for someone to bring love and joy to a homestead that's been dominated by men for a decade. But when he convinces Heidi to come clean the cowboy cabins, she changes all that. But the siren's call of a bakery is still loud in Heidi's ears, even if she's also seeing a future with Frank. Can she rely on her faith in ways she's never had to before or will their relationship end when summer does?

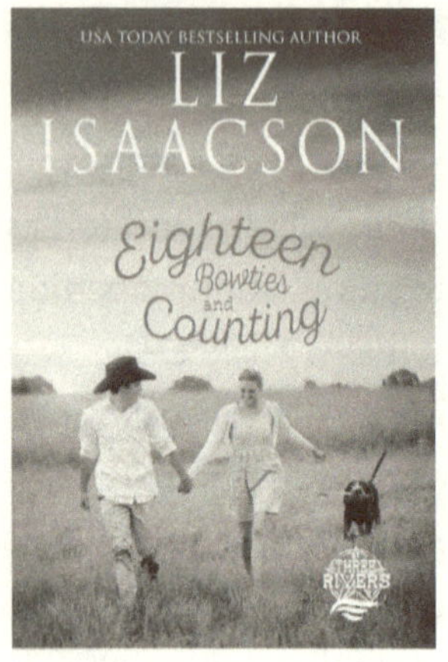

Eighteen Bowties and Counting: A Three Rivers Ranch Romance™ (Book 18): He's her older brother's best friend and completely off-limits. She's got a way with horses...and a heart condition. Can Beau and Charlotte navigate close quarters to find their happily-ever-after?

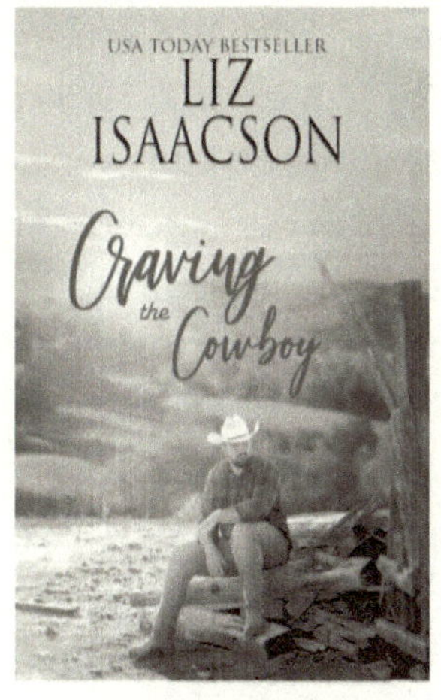

Craving the Cowboy (Book 1): Dwayne Carver is set to inherit his family's ranch in the heart of Texas Hill Country, and in order to keep up with his ranch duties and fulfill his dreams of owning a horse farm, he hires top trainer Felicity Lightburne. They get along great, and she can envision herself on this new farm—at least until her mother falls ill and she has to return to help her. Can Dwayne and Felicity work through their differences to find their happily-ever-after?

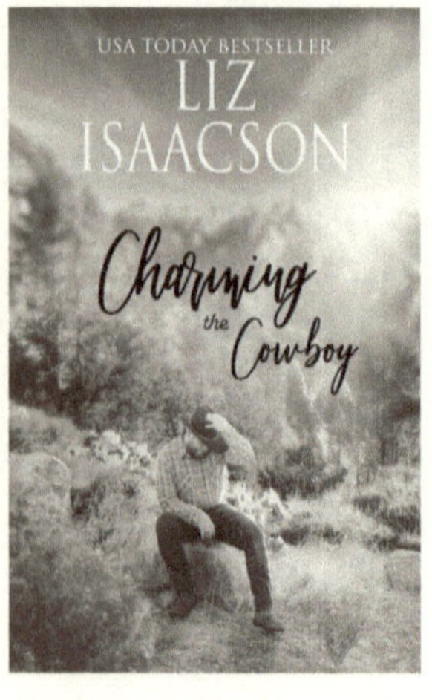

Charming the Cowboy (Book 2): Third grade teacher Heather Carver has had her eye on Levi Rhodes for a couple of years now, but he seems to be blind to her attempts to charm him. When she breaks her arm while on his horse ranch, Heather infiltrates Levi's life in ways he's never thought of, and his strict anti-female stance slips. Will Heather heal his emotional scars and he care for her physical ones so they can have a real relationship?

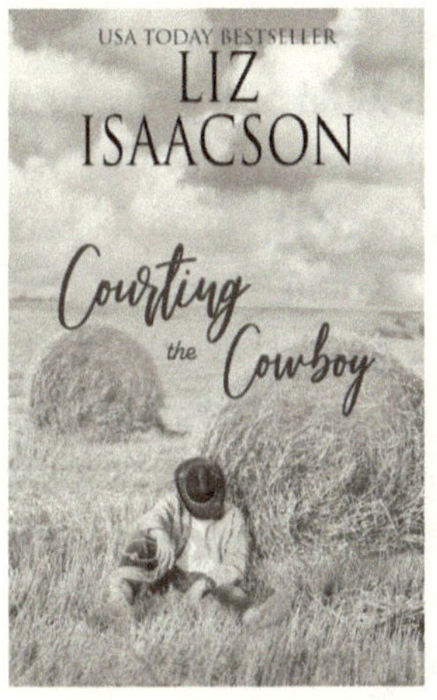

Courting the Cowboy (Book 3): Frustrated with the cowboy-only dating scene in Grape Seed Falls, May Sotheby joins Texas-Faithful.com, hoping to find her soul mate without having to relocate--or deal with cowboy hats and boots. She has no idea that Kurt Pemberton, foreman at Grape Seed Ranch, is the man she starts communicating with... Will May be able to follow her heart and get Kurt to forgive her so they can be together?

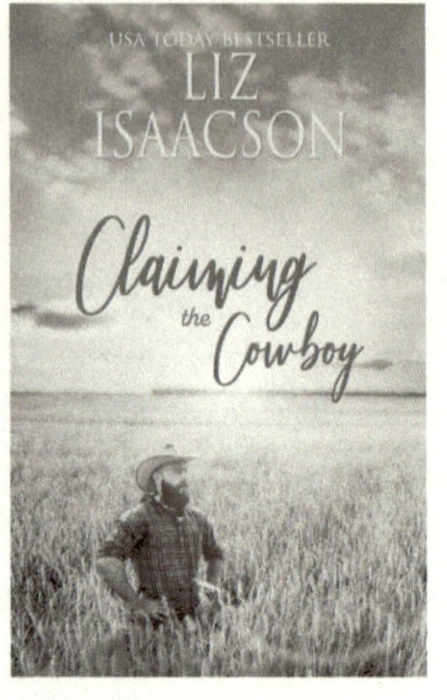

Claiming the Cowboy, Royal Brothers Book 1 (Grape Seed Falls Romance Book 4): Unwilling to be tied down, farrier Robin Cook has managed to pack her entire life into a two-hundred-and-eighty square-foot house, and that includes her Yorkie. Cowboy and co-foreman, Shane Royal has had his heart set on Robin for three years, even though she flat-out turned him down the last time he asked her to dinner. But she's back at Grape Seed Ranch for five weeks as she works her horseshoeing magic, and he's still interested, despite a bitter life lesson that left a bad taste for marriage in his mouth.

Robin's interested in him too. But can she find room for Shane in her tiny house--and can he take a chance on her with his tired heart?

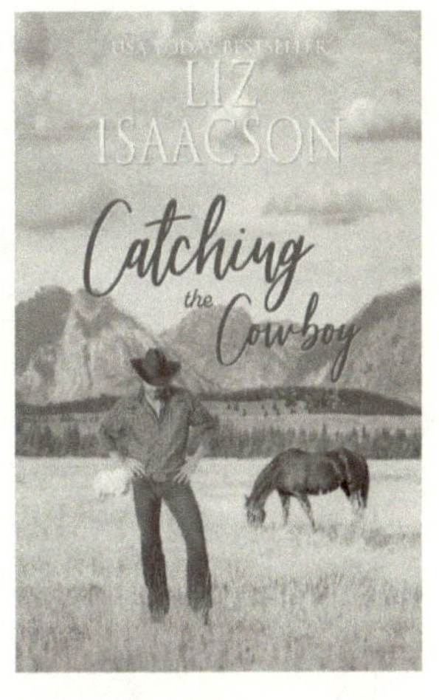

Catching the Cowboy, Royal Brothers Book 2 (Grape Seed Falls Romance Book 5): Dylan Royal is good at two things: whistling and caring for cattle. When his cows are being attacked by an unknown wild animal, he calls Texas Parks & Wildlife for help. He wasn't expecting a beautiful mammologist to show up, all flirty and fun and everything Dylan didn't know he wanted in his life.

Hazel Brewster has gone on more first dates than anyone in Grape Seed Falls, and she thinks maybe Dylan deserves a second... Can they find their way through wild animals, huge life changes, and their emotional pasts to find their forever future?

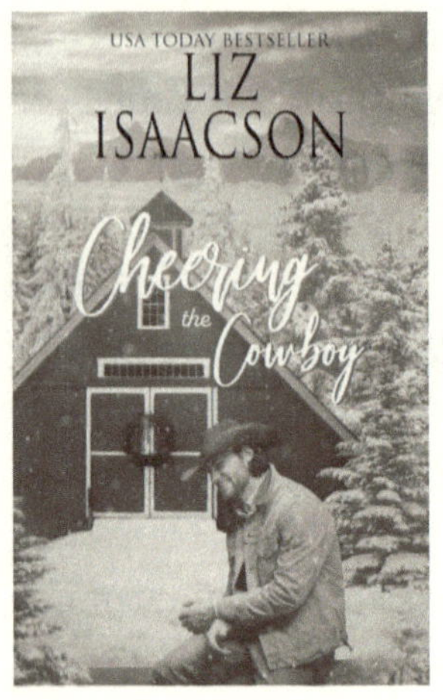

Cheering the Cowboy, Royal Brothers Book 3 (Grape Seed Falls Romance Book 6): Austin Royal loves his life on his new ranch with his brothers. But he doesn't love that Shayleigh Hatch came with the property, nor that he has to take the blame for the fact that he now owns her childhood ranch. They rarely have a conversation that doesn't leave him furious and frustrated--and yet he's still attracted to Shay in a strange, new way.

Shay inexplicably likes him too, which utterly confuses and angers her. As they work to make this Christmas the best the Triple Towers Ranch has ever seen, can they also navigate through their rocky relationship to smoother waters?

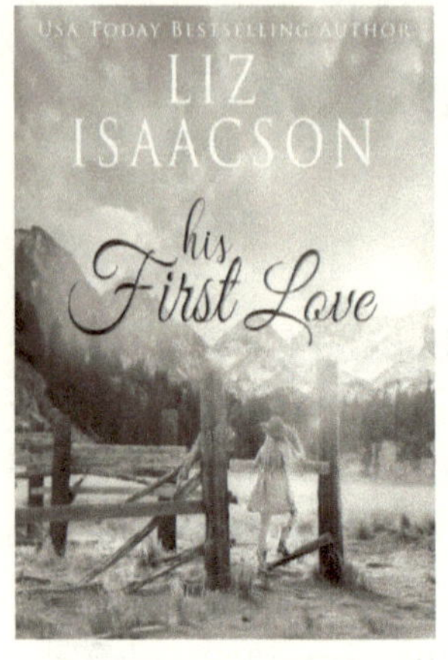

His First Love (Book 1): She broke up with him a decade ago. He's back in town after finishing a degree at MIT, ready to start his job at the family company. Can Hunter and Molly find their way through their pasts to build a future together?

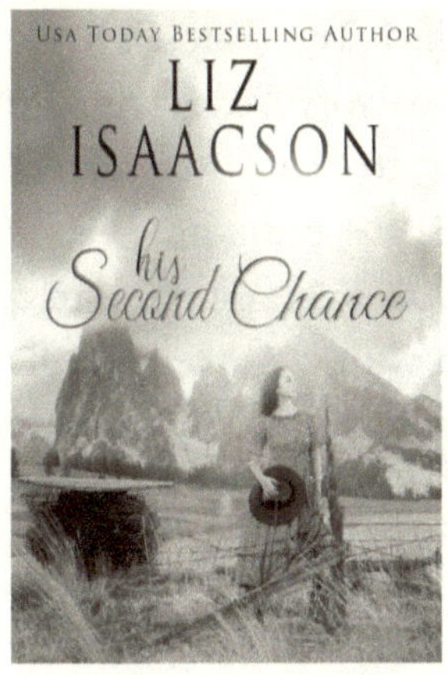

His Second Chance (Book 2): They broke up over twenty years ago. She's lost everything when she shows up at the farm in Ivory Peaks where he works. Can Matt and Gloria heal from their pasts to find a future happily-ever-after with each other?

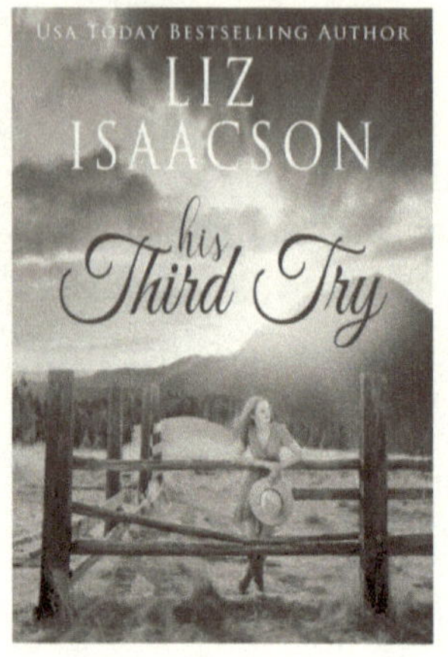

His Third Try (Book 3): He moved to Ivory Peaks with his daughter to start over after a devastating break-up. She's never had a meaningful relationship with a man, especially a cowboy. Can Boone and Cosette help each other heal enough to build a happily-ever-after...and a family?

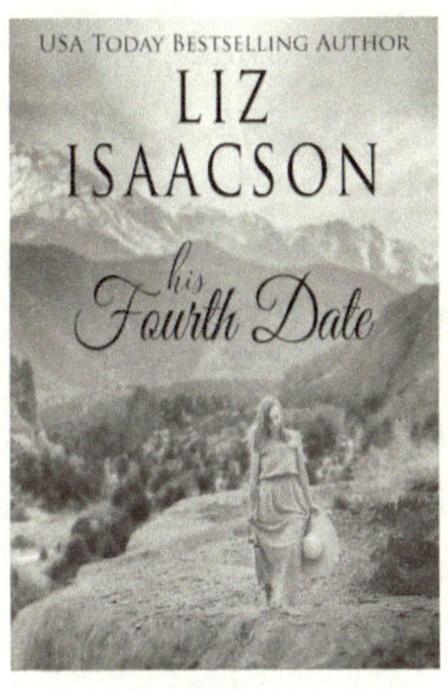

His Fourth Date (Book 4): Their relationship has been nothing but loose goats, a leaking roof, and her complete humiliation after he pays her mortgage so she won't lose her farm. Travis wants to go back in time and start over with Poppy, but he doesn't know how. Can a small town speed-dating event get their second chance off on the right foot?

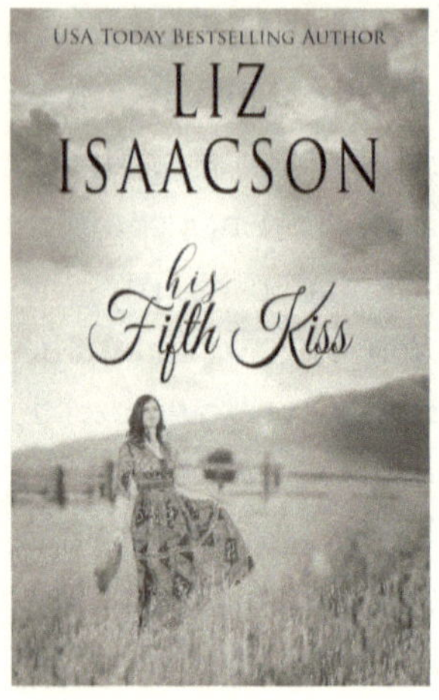

His Fifth Kiss (Book 5): They once had a few summers together. Now, Michael Hammond is back in town after a devastating injury overseas. He's looking to reset and recover...not to fall in love. But with Gertrude Whettstein also back at the farm, can Gerty and Mike make their second chance romance into a happily-ever-after?

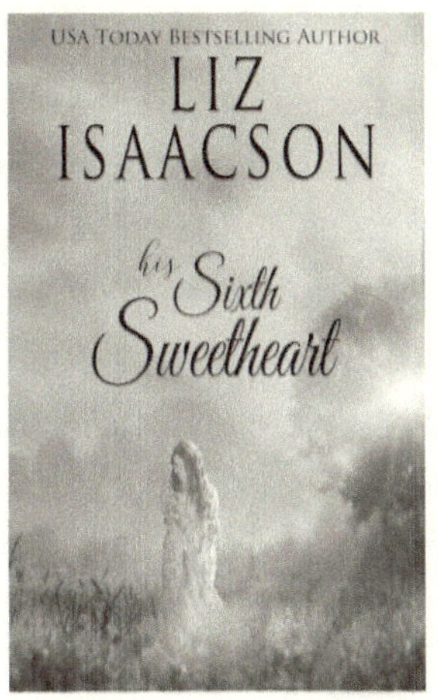

His Sixth Sweetheart (Book 6): She's had a crush on him for decades. He's finally in a place where he feels ready to date the boss's daughter. Can Cord and Jane take their relationship to the next level without getting burned?

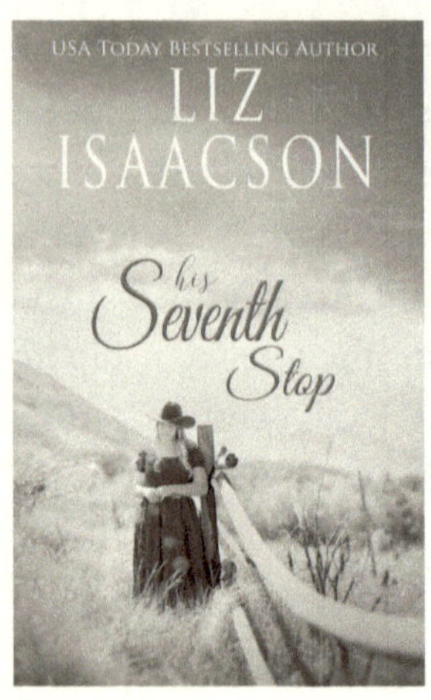

His Seventh Stop (Book 7): He's a seasoned cowboy on a delivery mission. She's a resilient hobby farm owner braving the winter storm. Can Keith and Lindsay forge a bond in the heart of a tempest and find love in the calm that follows?

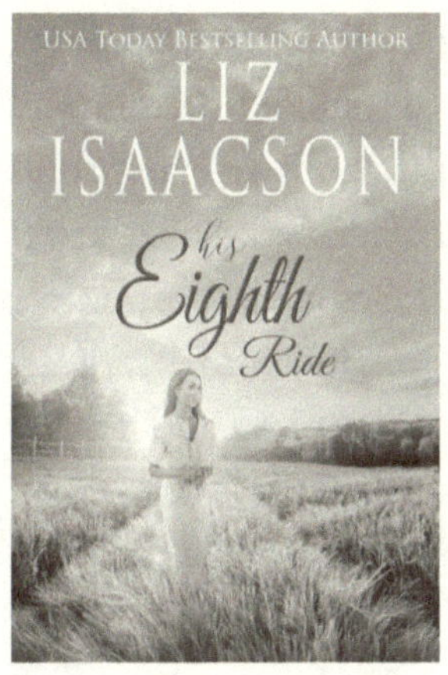

His Eighth Ride (Book 8): Tag has secretly admired Opal from afar. He even went so far as to ask her out, but the timing was all off, and now he's just awkward around his best friend's little sister. Can their unexpected reunion mend the fences between them and finally lead them to the forever love they've been waiting for?

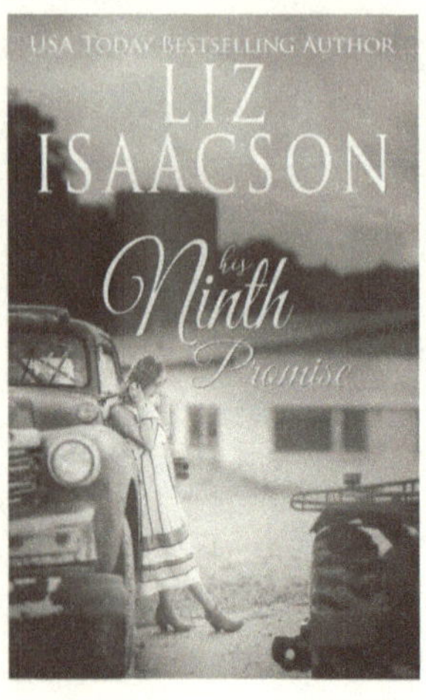

His Ninth Promise (Book 9): At home on the Hammond Family Farm, where gypsy souls and rodeo dreams collide, Tucker's heart has been beating for Bobbie Jo. But with her heart set on a distant love and Tucker searching for something more, their paths seemed destined to cross but never converge. Can he stick it out for another ride if the promise is coming home to Bobbie Jo?

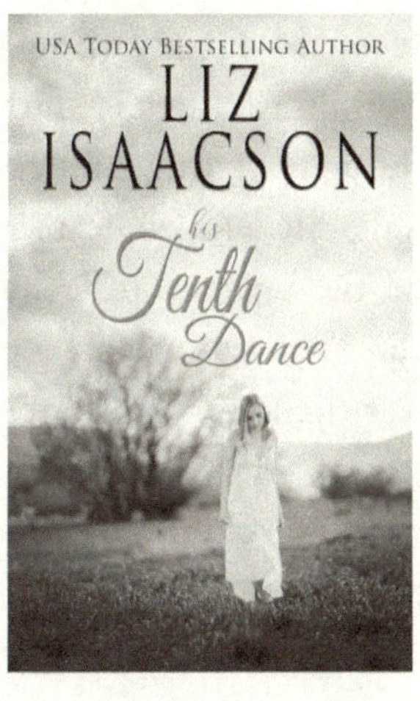

His Tenth Dance (Book 10): Mission has carried the weight of his past for a long time, and letting someone in feels like a risk. But maybe, just maybe, Kristie is worth it. When his granddad tells her about his secret crush, sparks fly between them, walls come down, and love might just get a second chance to take the lead... if Kristie and Mission are willing to take a leap of faith.

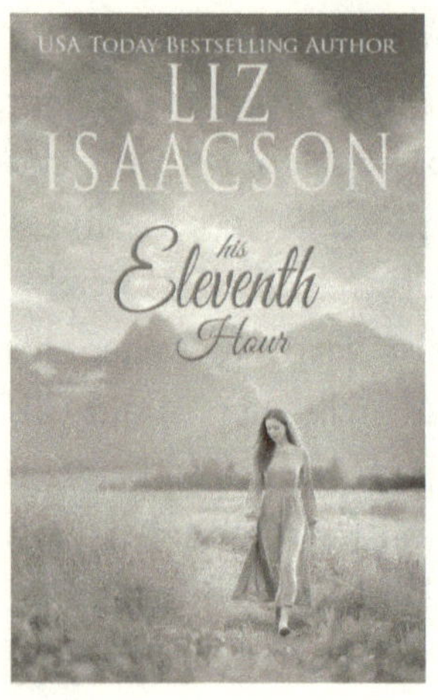

His Eleventh Hour (Book 11): Champion bull rider Tarr Olson thought getting injured and losing his rodeo career would be the biggest challenge he'd face. That was before he met his neighbor—the beautiful but ice-cold veterinarian who wants nothing to do with him.

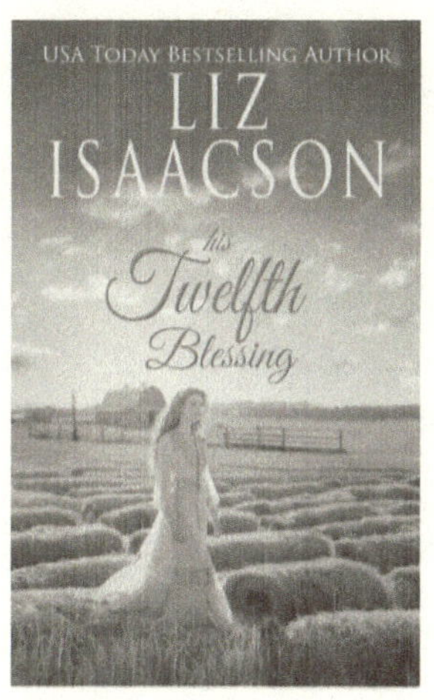

His Twelfth Blessing (Book 12): He's a grumpy cowboy billionaire who lives for the family farm. She's a brilliant agricultural consultant who never stays in one place. Can Deacon and Chapelle find their forever home together?

About Liz

Liz Isaacson writes inspirational romance, usually set in Texas, or Wyoming, or anywhere else horses and cowboys exist. She lives in Utah, where she writes full-time, takes her two dogs to the park everyday, and eats a lot of veggies while writing. Find her on her website at feelgoodfiction-books.com